Books by Elmore Leonard

ELMORE LEONARD

Forty Lashes Less One

HARPER

An Imprint of HarperCollinsPublishers

HARPER

An Imprint of HarperCollins*Publishers*
10 East 53rd Street
New York, New York 10022-5299

First Harper mass market printing: August 2011
First HarperTorch paperback printing: November 2002

HarperCollins® and Harper® are registered trademarks of HarperCollins Publishers.

Printed in the United States of America

10 9 8 7 6 5 4

Forty Lashes Less One

1

The train was late and didn't get into Yuma until after dark. Then the ticket agent at the depot had to telephone the prison and tell them they had better get some transportation down here. He had three people waiting on a ride up the hill: a man he had never seen before who said he was the new prison superintendent, and another man he knew was a deputy sheriff from Pima County and he had a prisoner with him, handcuffed, a big colored boy.

Whoever it was on the phone up at the prison said they had sent a man two hours ago and if the train had been on time he would have met them. The ticket agent said well, they were here now and somebody better hurry with the transportation, because the Southern Pacific didn't care for convicts hanging around the depot, even if the boy was handcuffed.

The Pima deputy said hell, it wasn't anything new; every time he delivered a man he had to sit and wait on the prison people to get off their ass. He asked the big colored boy if he minded waiting, sitting in a nice warm train depot, or would he rather be up there in one of

1

them carved-out cells with the wind whistling in across the river? The Pima deputy said something about sweating all day and freezing at night; but the colored boy, whose name was Harold Jackson, didn't seem to be listening.

The new prison superintendent—the new, temporary superintendent—Mr. Everett Manly, heard him. He nodded, and adjusted his gold-frame glasses. He said yes, he was certainly familiar with Arizona winters, having spent seven years at the Chiricahua Apache Mission School. Mr. Manly heard himself speak and it sounded all right. It sounded natural.

On the train Mr. Manly had exchanged a few words with the deputy, but had not spoken to the colored boy. He could have asked him his name and where he was from; he could have asked him about his sentence and told him that if he behaved himself he would be treated fairly. He could have asked him if he wanted to pray. But with the Pima deputy sitting next to the colored boy—all afternoon and evening on the wicker seats, bumping and swaying, looking out at the sun haze on the desert and the distant, dark brown mountains—Mr. Manly had not been able to get the first words out, to start a conversation. He was not afraid of the colored boy, who could have been a cold-blooded killer for all he knew. It was the idea of the deputy sitting there listening that bothered him.

He thought about starting a friendly conversation with the ticket agent: ask him if he ever got up to the prison, or if he knew the superintendent, Mr. Rynning, who was in Florence at the present time seeing to the construction of the new penitentiary. He could say, "Well, it won't be long now, there won't be any more Yuma Territorial Prison," and kidding, add, "I suppose you'll be sorry to see it closed." Except maybe he wasn't supposed to talk about it in idle conversation. It had been mentioned in newspapers—"Hell-Hole on the Bluff to Open Its Doors Forever by the Spring of 1909"—pretty clever, saying *opening* its doors instead of closing them. And no doubt the station agent knew all about it. Living here he would have to. But a harmless conversation could start false rumors and speculation, and before you knew it somebody from the Bureau would write and ask how come he was going around telling everybody about official government business.

If the ticket agent brought up the subject that would be different. He could be noncommittal. "You heard the old prison's closing, huh? Well, after thirty-three years I imagine you won't be too sorry to see it happen." But the ticket agent didn't bring up the subject.

A little while later they heard the noise outside. The ticket agent looked at them through his barred window and said, "There's a motor conveyance pulling into the yard I reckon is for you people."

Mr. Manly had never ridden in an automobile before. He asked the driver what kind it was and the driver told him it was a twenty-horsepower Ford Touring Car, powerful and speedy, belonged to the superintendent, Mr. Rynning. It was comfortable, Mr. Manly said, but kind of noisy, wasn't it? He wanted to ask how much a motor rig like this cost, but there was the prison above him: the walls and the guard towers against the night sky, the towers, like little houses with pointed roofs; dark houses, nobody home. When the gravel road turned and climbed close along the south wall, Mr. Manly had to look almost straight up, and he said to the guard driving the car, "I didn't picture the walls so high." And the guard answered, "Eighteen feet up and eight feet thick. A man can't jump it and he can't bore through neither.

"My last trip up this goddamn rock pile," the Pima deputy said, sitting in the back seat with his prisoner. "I'm going to the railroad hotel and get me a bottle of whiskey and in the morning I'm taking the train home and ain't never coming back here again."

The rest of the way up the hill Mr. Manly said nothing. He would remember this night and the strange feeling of riding in a car up Prison Hill, up close to this great silent mound of adobe and granite. Yuma Territorial Prison, that he had heard stories about for years—that he could almost reach out and touch. But was it like a prison? More like a tomb of an ancient king, Mr. Manly was thinking. A pyramid. A ghostly monument. Or, if it was a prison, then one that was already deserted. Inside the walls there were more than a hundred men. Maybe a hundred and fifty counting the guards. But there was no sound or sign of life, only this motor car putt-putting up the hill, taking forever to reach the top.

What if it did take forever, Mr. Manly thought. What if they kept going and going and never reached the prison gate, but kept moving up into stoney darkness for all eternity—until the four of them realized this was God's judgment upon them. (He could hear the Pima

4

deputy cursing and saying, "Now, wait a minute, I'm just here to deliver a prisoner!") It could happen this way, Mr. Manly thought. Who said you had to die first? Or, how did a person know when he was dead? Maybe he had died on the train. He had dozed off and opened his eyes as they were pulling into the depot—

A man sixty years old could die in his sleep. But—and here was the question—if he was dead and this was happening, why would he be condemned to darkness? What had he done wrong in his life?

Not even thinking about it very hard, he answered at once, though quietly: What have you done right? Sixty years of life, Mr. Manly thought. Thirty years as a preacher of the Holy Word, seven years as a missionary among pagan Indians. Half his life spent in God's service, and he was not sure he had converted even one soul to the Light of Truth.

They reached the top of the bluff at the west end of the prison and, coming around the corner, Mr. Manly saw the buildings that were set back from the main gate, dim shapes and cold yellow lights that framed windows and reflected on the hard-packed yard. He was aware of the buildings and thought briefly of an army post, single- and two-story structures with peaked roofs and neatly painted verandas. He heard the driver point out the guard's mess and recreation hall, the arsenal, the stable, the storehouses; he heard him say, "If you're staying in the sup'rintendent's cottage, it's over yonder by the trees."

Mr. Manly was familiar with government buildings in cleanswept areas. He had seen them at the San Carlos reservation and at Fort Huachuca and at the Indian School. He was staring at the prison wall where a single light showed the main gate as an oval cavern in the pale stone, a dark tunnel entrance crisscrossed with strips of iron.

The driver looked at Mr. Manly. After a moment he said, "The sally port. It's the only way in and, I guarantee, the only way out."

Bob Fisher, the turnkey, stood waiting back of the inner gate with two of his guards. He seemed either patient or half asleep, a solemn-looking man with a heavy, drooping mustache. He didn't have them open the iron lattice door until Mr. Manly and the Pima deputy and his prisoner were within the dark enclosure of the sally port and the outer gate was bolted and locked behind them. Then he gave a sign to open up and waited for them to step into the yard light.

The Pima deputy was pulling a folded sheaf of papers out of his coat pocket, dragging along his handcuffed prisoner. "I got a boy name of Harold Jackson wants to live with you the next fifteen years." He handed the papers to the turnkey and fished in his pants pocket for the keys to the handcuffs.

Bob Fisher unfolded the papers close to his stomach and glanced at the first sheet. "We'll take care of him," he said, and folded the papers again.

Mr. Manly stood by waiting, holding his suitcase.

"I'll tell you what," the Pima deputy said. "I'll let you buy me a cup of coffee 'fore I head back."

"We'll see if we got any," Fisher said.

The Pima deputy had removed the handcuffs from the prisoner and was slipping them into his coat pocket. "I don't want to put you to any trouble," he said. "Jesus, a nice friendly person like you."

"You won't put us to any trouble," Fisher answered. His voice was low, and he seemed to put no effort or feeling into his words.

Mr. Manly kept waiting for the turnkey to notice him and greet him and have one of the guards take his suitcase; but the man stood at the edge of the yard light and didn't seem to look at any of them directly, though maybe he was looking at the prisoner, telling him with the sound of his voice that he didn't kid with anybody. What does he look like, Mr. Manly was thinking. He lowered his suitcase to the ground.

A streetcar motorman, that was it. With his gray guard uniform and gray uniform hat, the black shiny peak straight over his eyes. A tough old motorman with a sour stomach and a sour outlook from living within the confinement of a prison too many years. A man who never spoke if he didn't have to and only smiled about twice a year. The way the man's big mustache covered the sides of his mouth it would be hard to tell if he ever smiled at all.

Bob Fisher told one of the guards to take the Pima deputy over to the mess hall, then changed his mind and said no, take him outside to the guard's mess. The Pima deputy shrugged; he didn't care where he got his coffee. He took time to look at Mr. Manly and say, "Good luck,

7

mister." As Mr. Manly said, "Good luck to you too," not looking at the turnkey now but feeling him there, the Pima deputy turned his back on them; he waited to get through the double gates and was gone.

"My name is Everett Manly," Mr. Manly said. "I expect—"

But Fisher wasn't ready for him yet. He motioned to the guards and watched as they led the prisoner off toward a low, one-room adobe. Mr. Manly waited, also watching them. He could see the shapes of buildings in the darkness of the yard, here and there a light fixed above a doorway. Past the corner of a two-story building, out across the yard, was the massive outline of a long, windowless adobe with a light above its crisscrossed iron door. Probably the main cellblock. But in the darkness he couldn't tell about the other buildings, or make any sense of the prison's layout. He had the feeling again that the place was deserted except for the turnkey and the two guards.

"I understand you've come here to take charge."

All the waiting and the man had surprised him. But all was forgiven, because the man was looking at him now, acknowledging his presence.

"I'm Everett Manly. I expect Mr. Rynning wrote you I was coming. You're—"

"Bob Fisher, turnkey."

Mr. Manly smiled. "I guess you would be the man in charge of the keys." Showing him he had a sense of humor.

"I've been in charge of the whole place since Mr. Rynning's been gone."

"Well, I'm anxious to see everything and get to work." Mr. Manly was being sincere now, and humble. "I'm going to admit though, I haven't had much experience."

In his flat tone, Fisher said, "I understand you haven't had any."

Mr. Manly wished they weren't standing here alone. "No *prison* experience, that's true. But I've dealt with people all my life, Mr. Fisher, and nobody's told me yet convicts aren't people." He smiled again, still humble and willing to learn.

"Nobody will have to tell you," Fisher said. "You'll find out yourself."

He turned and walked off toward the one-room adobe. Mr. Manly had no choice but to pick up his suitcase and follow—Lord, with the awful feeling again and wishing he hadn't put so many books in with his clothes; the suitcase weighed a ton and he probably looked like an idiot walking with quick little steps and the thing banging against his leg. And then he was grateful and felt good again, because Bob Fisher was holding the door open for him and let him go inside first, into the lighted room where the colored boy was jackknifed over a table without any clothes on and the two guards were standing on either side of him.

One of the guards pulled him up and turned him around by the arm as Fisher closed the door. "He's clean," the guard said. "Nothing hid away down him or up him."

"He needs a hosing is all," the other guard said.

Fisher came across the plank floor, his eyes on the prisoner. "He ain't worked up a sweat yet."

9

"Jesus," the first guard said, "don't get close to him. He stinks to high heaven."

Mr. Manly put down his suitcase. "That's a long dusty train ride, my friend." Then, smiling a little, he added, "I wouldn't mind a bath myself."

The two guards looked over at him, then at Fisher, who was still facing the prisoner. "That's your new boss," Fisher said, "come to take Mr. Rynning's place while he's gone. See he gets all the bath water he wants. This boy here washes tomorrow with the others, after he's put in a day's work."

Mr. Manly said, "I didn't intend that to sound like I'm interfering with your customs or regulations—"

Fisher looked over at him now, waiting.

"I only meant it was sooty and dirty aboard the train."

Fisher waited until he was sure Mr. Manly had nothing more to say. Then he turned his attention to the prisoner again. One of the guards was handing the man a folded uniform and a broad-brimmed sweat-stained hat. Fisher watched him as he put the clothes on the table, shook open the pants and stepped into them: faded, striped gray and white convict pants that were short and barely reached to the man's high-top shoes. While he was buttoning up, Fisher opened the sheaf of papers the Pima deputy had given him, his gaze holding on the first sheet. "It says here you're Harold Jackson."

"Yes-suh, captain."

The Negro came to attention as Fisher looked up, a hint of surprise in his solemn expression. He seemed to study the prisoner more closely now and took his time before saying, "You ain't ever been here before, but you been somewhere. Where was it you served time, boy?"

"Fort Leavenworth, captain."

"You were in the army?"

"Yes-suh, captain."

"I never knew a nigger that was in the army. How long were you in it?"

"Over in Cuba eight months, captain. At Leavenworth four years hard labor."

"Well, they learned you some manners," Fisher said, "but they didn't learn you how to stay out of prison, did they? These papers say you killed a man. Is that right?"

"Yes-suh, captain."

"What'd you kill him with?"

"I hit him with a piece of pipe, captain."

"You robbing him?"

"No-suh, captain, we jes' fighting."

Mr. Manly cleared his throat. The pause held, and he said quickly, "Coming here he never gave the deputy any trouble, not once."

Fisher took his time as he looked around. He said, "I generally talk to a new man and find out who he is or who he believes he is, and we get a few things straightened out at the start." He paused. "If it's all right with you."

"Please go ahead," Mr. Manly said. "I just wanted to say he never acted smart on the trip, or was abusive. I doubt he said more than a couple words."

"That's fine." Fisher nodded patiently before looking at Harold Jackson again. "You're our last nigger," he said to him. "You're the only one we got now, and we

11

want you to be a good boy and work hard and do whatever you're told. Show you we mean it, we're going to help you out at first, give you something to keep you out of trouble."

There was a wooden box underneath the table. Mr. Manly didn't notice it until one of the guards stooped down and, with the rattling sound of chains, brought out a pair of leg-irons and a ball-peen hammer.

Mr. Manly couldn't hold back. "But he hasn't done anything yet!"

"No, sir," Bob Fisher said, "and he ain't about to with chains on his legs." He came over to Mr. Manly and, surprising him, picked up his suitcase and moved him through the door, closing it firmly behind them.

Outside, Fisher paused. "I'll get somebody to tote your bag over to Mr. Rynning's cottage. I expect you'll be most comfortable there."

"I appreciate it."

"Take your bath if you want one, have something to eat and a night's sleep—there's no sense in showing you around now—all right?"

"What are you going to do to the colored boy?"

"We're going to put him in a cell, if that's all right."

"But the leg-irons."

"He'll wear them a week. See what they feel like."

"I guess I'm just not used to your ways," Mr. Manly said. "I mean prison ways." He could feel the silence again among the darkened stone buildings and high walls. The turnkey walked off toward the empty, lighted area by the main gate. Mr. Manly had to step quickly to catch up with him. "I mean I believe a man should have a chance to prove himself first," he said, "before he's judged."

"They're judged before they get here."

"But putting leg-irons on them—"

"Not all of them. Just the ones I think need them, so they'll know what irons feel like."

Mr. Manly knew what he wanted to say, but he didn't have the right words. "I mean, don't they hurt terrible?"

"I sure hope so," Fisher answered.

As they came to the lighted area, a guard leaning against the iron grill of the gate straightened and adjusted his hat. Fisher let the guard know he had seen him, then stopped and put down the suitcase.

"This Harold Jackson," Fisher said. "Maybe you didn't hear him. He killed a man. He didn't miss Sunday school. He beat a man to death with an iron pipe."

"I know—I heard him."

"That's the kind of people we get here. Lot of them. They come in, we don't know what's on their minds. We don't know if they're going to behave or cause trouble or try and run or try and kill somebody else."

"I understand that part all right."

"Some of them we got to show right away who's running this place."

Mr. Manly was frowning. "But this boy Harold Jackson, he seemed all right. He was polite, said yes-sir to you. Why'd you put leg-irons on him?"

Now it was Fisher's turn to look puzzled. "You saw him same as I did."

"I don't know what you mean."

"I mean he's a nigger, ain't he?"

Looking up at the turnkey, Mr. Manly's gold-frame spectacles glistened in the overhead light. "You're saying that's the only reason you put leg-irons on him?"

"If I could tell all the bad ones," Bob Fisher said, "as easy as I can tell a nigger, I believe I'd be sup'rintendent."

Jesus Christ, the man was even dumber than he looked. He could have told him a few more things: sixteen years at Yuma, nine years as turnkey, and he hadn't seen a nigger yet who didn't need to wear irons or spend some time in the snake den. It was the way they were, either lazy or crazy; you had to beat 'em to make 'em work, or chain 'em to keep 'em in line. He would like to see just one good nigger. Or one good, hard-working Indian for that matter. Or a Mexican you could trust. Or a preacher who knew enough to keep his nose in church and out of other people's business.

Bob Fisher had been told two weeks earlier, in a letter from Mr. Rynning, that an acting superintendent would soon be coming to Yuma.

Mr. Rynning's letter had said: "Not an experienced penal administrator, by the way, but, of all things, a preacher, an ordained minister of the Holy Word Church who has been wrestling with devils in Indian schools for several years and evidently feels qualified to match his strength against convicts. This is not my doing. Mr. Manly's name came to me through the Bureau as someone who, if not eminently qualified, is at least conveniently located and willing to take the job on a temporary basis. (The poor fellow must be desperate.

Or, perhaps misplaced and the Bureau doesn't know what else to do with him but send him to prison, out of harm's way.) He has had some administrative experience and, having worked on an Apache reservation, must know something about inventory control and logistics. The bureau insists on an active administrator at Yuma while, in the same breath, they strongly suggest I remain in Florence during the new prison's final stage of preparation. Hence, you will be meeting your new superintendent in the very near future. Knowing you will oblige him with your utmost cooperation I remain . . ."

Mr. Rynning remained in Florence while Bob Fisher remained in Yuma with a Holy Word Pentacostal preacher looking over his shoulder.

The clock on the wall of the superintendent's office said ten after nine. Fisher, behind the big mahogany desk, folded Mr. Rynning's letter and put it in his breast pocket. After seeing Mr. Manly through the gate, he had come up here to pick up his personal file. No sense in leaving anything here if the preacher was going to occupy the office. The little four-eyed son of a bitch, maybe a few days here would scare hell out of him and run him back to Sunday school. Turning in the swivel chair, Fisher could see the reflection of the room in the darkened window glass and could see himself sitting at the desk; with a thumb and first finger he smoothed his mustache and continued to fool with it as he looked at the clock again.

Still ten after nine. He was off duty; had been since six. Had waited two hours for the preacher.

It was too early to go home: his old lady would still be

15

up and he'd have to look at her and listen to her talk for an hour or more. Too early to go home, and too late to watch the two women convicts take their bath in the cook shack. They always finished and were gone by eight-thirty, quarter to nine. He had been looking forward to watching them tonight, especially Norma Davis. Jesus, she had big ones, and a nice round white fanny. The Mexican girl was smaller, like all the Mexican girls he had ever seen; she was all right, though; especially with the soapy water on her brown skin. It was a shame; he hadn't watched them in about four nights. If the train had been on time he could have met the preacher and still got over to the cook shack before eight-thirty. It was like the little son of a bitch's train to be late. There was something about him, something that told Fisher the man couldn't do anything right, and would mess up anything he took part in.

Tomorrow he'd show him around and answer all his dumb questions.

Tonight—he could stare at the clock for an hour and go home.

He could stare out at the empty yard and hope for something to happen. He could pull a surprise inspection of the guard posts, maybe catch somebody sleeping.

He could stop at a saloon on the way home. Or go down to Frank Shelby's cell, No. 14, and buy a pint of tequila off him.

What Bob Fisher did, he pulled out the papers on the new prisoner, Harold Jackson, and started reading about him.

* * *

One of the guards asked Harold Jackson if he'd ever worn leg-irons before. Sitting tired, hunch-shouldered on the floor, he said yeah. They looked down at him and he looked up at them, coming full awake but not showing it, and said yes-suh, he believed it was two times. That's all, if the captain didn't count the prison farm. He'd wore irons there because they liked everybody working outside the jail to wear irons. It wasn't on account he had done anything.

The guard said all right, that was enough. They give him a blanket and took him shuffling across the dark yard to the main cell block, then through the iron-cage gate where bare overhead lights showed the stone passageway and the cell doors on both sides. The guards didn't say anything to him. They stopped at Cell No. 8, unlocked the door, pushed him inside, and clanged the ironwork shut behind him.

As their steps faded in the passageway, Harold Jackson could make out two tiers of bunks and feel the closeness of the walls and was aware of a man breathing in his sleep. He wasn't sure how many were in this cell. He let his eyes get used to the darkness before he took a step, then another, the leg chains clinking in the silence. The back wall wasn't three steps away. The bunks, three decks high on both sides of him, were close enough to touch. Which would make this a six-man room, he figured, about eight feet by nine feet. Blanket-covered shapes lay close to him in the middle bunks. He couldn't make out the top ones and didn't want to feel around;

17

but he could see the bottom racks were empty. Harold Jackson squatted on the floor and ducked into the right-side bunk.

The three-tiered bunks and the smell of the place reminded him of the troopship, though it had been awful hot down in the hold. Ten days sweating down in that dark hold while the ship was tied up at Tampa and they wouldn't let any of the Negro troops go ashore, not even to walk the dock and stretch their legs. He never did learn the name of that ship, and he didn't care. When they landed at Siboney, Harold Jackson walked off through the jungle and up into the hills. For two weeks he stayed with a Cuban family and ate sugar cane and got a kick out of how they couldn't speak any English, though they were Negro, same as he was. When he had rested and felt good he returned to the base and they threw him in the stockade. They said he was a deserter. He said he came back, didn't he? They said he was still a deserter.

He had never been in a cell that was this cold. Not even at Leavenworth. Up there in the Kansas winter the cold times were in the exercise yard, stamping your feet and moving to keep warm; the cell was all right, maybe a little cold sometimes. That was a funny thing, most of the jails he remembered as being hot: the prison farm wagon that was like a circus cage and the city jails and the army stockade in Cuba. He'd be sitting on a bench sweating or laying in the rack sweating, slapping mosquitoes, scratching, or watching the cockroaches fooling around and running nowhere. Cockroaches never looked like they knew where they were going. No, the heat was all right. The heat, the bugs were like part of being in jail. The cold was something he would have to get used to. Pretend it was hot. Pretend he was in Cuba. If he had to pick a jail to be in, out of all the places—if somebody said, "You got to go to jail for ten years, but we let you pick the place"—he'd pick the stockade at Siboney. Not because it was a good jail, but because it was in Cuba, and Cuba was a nice-looking place, with the ocean and the trees and plenty of shade. That's a long way away, Harold Jackson said to himself. You ain't going to see it again.

There wasn't any wind. The cold just lay over him and didn't go away. His body was all right; it was his feet and his hands. Harold Jackson rolled to his side to reach down below the leg-irons that dug hard into his ankles and work his shoes off, then put his hands, palms together like he was praying, between the warmth of his legs. There was no use worrying about where he was. He would think of Cuba and go to sleep.

In the morning, in the moments before opening his eyes, he wasn't sure where he was. He was confused because a minute ago he'd have sworn he'd been holding a piece of sugar cane, the purple peeled back in knife strips and he was sucking, chewing the pulp to draw out the sweet juice. But he wasn't holding any cane now, and he wasn't in Cuba.

The bunk jiggled, strained, and moved back in place as somebody got down from above him. There were sounds of movement in the small cell, at least two men.

19

"You don't believe it, take a look."

"Jesus Christ," another voice said, a younger voice. "What's he doing in here?"

Both of them white voices. Harold Jackson could feel them standing between the bunks. He opened his eyes a little bit at a time until he was looking at prison-striped legs. It wasn't much lighter in the cell than before, when he'd gone to sleep, but he could see the stripes all right and he knew that outside it was morning.

A pair of legs swung down from the opposite bunk and hung there, wool socks and yellow toenails poking out of holes. "What're you looking at?" this one said, his voice low and heavy with sleep.

"We got a coon in here with us," the younger voice said.

The legs came down and the space was filled with faded, dirty convict stripes. Harold Jackson turned his head a little and raised his eyes. His gaze met theirs as they hunched over to look at him, studying him as if he was something they had never seen before. There was a heavy-boned, beard-stubbled face; a blond baby-boy face; and a skinny, slick-haired face with a big cavalry mustache that drooped over the corners of the man's mouth.

"Somebody made a mistake," the big man said. "In the dark."

"Joe Dean seen him right away."

"I smelled him," the one with the cavalry mustache said.

"Jesus," the younger one said now, "wait till Shelby finds out."

Harold Jackson came out of the bunk, rising slowly, uncoiling and bringing up his shoulders to stand eye to eye with the biggest of the three. He stared at the man's dead-looking deep-set eyes and at the hairs sticking out of a nose that was scarred and one time had been broken. "You gentlemen excuse me," Harold Jackson said, moving past the young boy and the one who was called Joe Dean. He stood with his back to them and aimed at the slop bucket against the wall.

They didn't say anything at first; just stared at him. But as Harold Jackson started to go the younger one murmured, "Jesus Christ—" as if awed, or saying a prayer. He stared at Harold as long as he could, then broke for the door and began yelling through the ironwork, "Guard! Guard! Goddamn it, there's a nigger in here pissing in our toilet!"

2

Raymond San Carlos heard the sound of Junior's voice before he made out the words: somebody yelling—for a guard. Somebody gone crazy, or afraid of something. Something happening in one of the cells close by. He heard quick footsteps now, going past, and turned his head enough to look from his bunk to the door.

It was morning. The electric lights were off in the cell block and it was dark now, the way a barn with its doors open is dark. He could hear other voices now and footsteps and, getting louder, the metal-ringing sound of the guards banging crowbars on the cell doors—good morning, get up and go to the toilet and put your shoes on and fold your blankets—the iron clanging coming closer, until it was almost to them and the convict above Raymond San Carlos yelled, "All right, we hear you! God Almighty—" The other convict in the cell, across from him in an upper bunk, said, "I'd like to wake them sons of bitches up some time." The man above Raymond said, "Break their goddamn eardrums." The other man said, "No, I'd empty slop pails on 'em." And the crow-

23

bar clanged against the door and was past them, banging, clanging down the passageway.

Another guard came along in a few minutes and unlocked each cell. Raymond was ready by the time he got to them, standing by the door to be first out. One of the convicts in the cell poked Raymond in the back and, when he turned around, pointed to the bucket.

"It ain't my turn," Raymond said.

"If I want you to empty it," the convict said, his partner close behind him, looking over his shoulder, "then it's your turn."

Raymond shrugged and they stood aside to let him edge past them. He could argue with them and they could pound his head against the stone wall and say he fell out of his bunk. He could pick up the slop bucket and say, "Hey," and when they turned around he could throw it at them. Thinking about it afterward would be good, but the getting beat up and pounded against the wall wouldn't be good. Or they might stick his face in a bucket. God, he'd get sick, and every time he thought of it after he'd get sick.

He had learned to hold onto himself and think ahead, looking at the good results and the bad results, and decide quickly if doing something was worth it. One time he hadn't held onto himself—the time he worked for the Sedona cattle people up on Oak Creek—and it was the reason he was here.

He had held on at first, for about a year while the other riders—some of them—kidded him about having a fancy name like Raymond San Carlos when he was Apache Indian down to the soles of his feet. Chiricahua

Apache, they said. Maybe a little taller than most, but look at them black beady eyes and the flat nose. Pure Indin.

The Sedona hands got tired of it after a while; all except two boys who wouldn't leave him alone: a boy named Buzz Moore and another one they called Eljay. They kept at him every day. One of them would say, "What's that in his hair?" and pretend to pick something out, holding it between two fingers and studying it closely. "Why, it's some fuzz off a turkey feather, must have got stuck there from his headdress." Sometimes when it was hot and dry one of these two would look up at the sky and say, "Hey, chief, commence dancing and see if you can get us some rain down here." They asked him if he ever thought about white women, which he would never in his life ever get to have. They'd drink whiskey in front of him and not give him any, saying it was against the law to give an Indian firewater. Things like that.

At first it hadn't been too hard to hold on and go along with the kidding. Riding for Sedona was a good job, and worth it. Raymond would usually grin and say nothing. A couple of times he tried to tell them he was American and only his name was Mexican. He had made up what he thought was a pretty good story.

"See, my father's name was Armando de San Carlos y Zamora. He was born in Mexico, I don't know where, but I know he come up here to find work and that's when he met my mother who's an American, Maria Ramirez, and they got married. So when I'm born here, I'm American too."

25

He remembered Buzz Moore saying, "Maria Ramirez? What kind of American name is that?"

The other one, Eljay, who never let him alone, said, "So are Apache Indins American if you want to call everybody who's born in this country American. But anybody knows Indins ain't citizens. And if you ain't a citizen, you ain't American." He said to Raymond, "You ever vote?"

"I ain't never been where there was anything to vote about," Raymond answered.

"You go to school?"

"A couple of years."

"Then you don't know anything about what is a U. S. citizen. Can you read and write?"

Raymond shook his head.

"There you are," Eljay said.

Buzz Moore said then, "His daddy could have been Indin. They got Indins in Mexico like anywhere else. Why old Geronimo himself lived down there and could have sired a whole tribe of little Indins."

And Eljay said, "You want to know the simple truth? He's Chiricahua Apache, born and reared on the San Carlos Indin reservation, and that's how he got his fancy name. Made it up so people wouldn't think he was Indin."

"Well," Buzz Moore said, "he could be some part Mexican."

"If that's so," Eljay said, "what we got here is a red greaser."

They got a kick out of that and called him the red greaser through the winter and into April—until the day up in the high meadows they were gathering spring calves and their mammas and chasing them down to the valley graze. They were using revolvers and shotguns part of the time to scare the stock out of the brush stands and box canyons and keep them moving. Raymond remembered the feel of the 12-gauge Remington, holding it pointed up with the stock tight against his thigh. He would fire it this way when he was chasing stock—aiming straight up—and would feel the Remington kick against his leg. He kept off by himself most of the day, enjoying the good feeling of being alone in high country. He remembered the day vividly: the clean line of the peaks towering against the sky, the shadowed canyons and the slopes spotted yellow with arrowroot blossoms. He liked the silence; he liked being here alone and not having to think about anything or talk to anybody.

It wasn't until the end of the day he realized how sore his leg was from the shotgun butt punching it. Raymond swung down off the sorrel he'd been riding and limped noticeably as he walked toward the cook fire. Eljay was standing there. Eljay took one look and said, "Hey, greaser, is that some kind of one-legged Indin dance you're doing?" Raymond stopped. He raised the Remington and shot Eljay square in the chest with both loads.

On this morning in February, 1909, as he picked up the slop bucket and followed his two cellmates out into the passageway. Raymond had served almost four years of a life sentence for second-degree murder.

The guard, R. E. Baylis, didn't lay his crowbar against No. 14, the last door at the east end of the cellblock. He

27

opened the door and stepped inside and waited for Frank Shelby to look up from his bunk.

"You need to be on the supply detail today?" R. E. Baylis asked.

"What's today?"

"Tuesday."

"Tomorrow," Shelby said. "What's it like out?"

"Bright and fair, going to be warm."

"Put me on an outside detail."

"We got a party building a wall over by the cemetery."

"Hauling the bricks?"

"Bricks already there."

"That'll be all right," Shelby said. He sat up, swinging his legs over the side of the bunk. He was alone in the cell, in the upper of a double bunk. The triple bunk opposite him was stacked with cardboard boxes and a wooden crate and a few canvas sacks. A shelf and mirror hung from the back wall. There was also a chair by the wall with a hole cut out of the seat and a bucket underneath. A roll of toilet paper rested on one of the arms. The convicts called the chair Shelby's throne. "Get somebody to empty the bucket, will you?" Looking at the guard again, Shelby said, "You need anything?"

R. E. Baylis touched his breast pocket. "Well, I guess I could use some chew."

"Box right by your head," Shelby said. "I got Mail Pouch and Red Man. Or I got some Copenhagen if you want."

R. E. Baylis fished a hand in the box. "I might as well take a couple—case I don't see you again today."

"You know where to find me." Shelby dropped to the floor, pulled on half-boots, hopping a couple of times to keep his balance, then ran a hand through his dark hair as he straightened up, standing now in his boots and long underwear. "I believe I was supposed to get a clean outfit today."

"Washing machine broke down yesterday."

"Tomorrow then for sure, uh?" Shelby had an easy, unhurried way of talking. It was known that he never raised his voice or got excited. They said the way you told if he was mad or irritated, he would fool with his mustache; he would keep smoothing it down with two fingers until he decided what had to be done and either did it himself or had somebody else do it. Frank Shelby was serving forty-five years for armed robbery and second-degree murder and had brought three of his men with him to Yuma, each of them found guilty on the same counts and serving thirty years apiece.

Junior was one of them. He banged through the cell door as Shelby was getting into his prison stripes, buttoning his coat. "You got your mean go-to-hell look on this morning," Shelby said. "Was that you yelling just now?"

"They stuck a nigger in our cell last night while we was asleep." Junior turned to nail the guard with his look, putting the blame on him.

"It wasn't me," R. E. Baylis said. "I just come on duty."

"You don't throw his black ass out, we will," Junior said. By Jesus, this was Worley Lewis, Jr. talking, nineteen-year-old convict going on forty-nine before he would ever see the outside of a penitentiary, but he was one of Frank Shelby's own and that said he could stand up to a guard and mouth him if he had a good enough reason. "I'm telling you, Soonzy'll kill the son of a bitch."

"I'll find out why—" the guard began.

"It was a mistake," Shelby said. "Put him in the wrong cell is all."

"He's in there now, great big buck. Joe Dean seen him first, woke me up, and I swear I couldn't believe my eyes."

Shelby went over to the mirror and picked up a comb from the shelf. "It's nothing to get upset about," he said, making a part and slanting the dark hair carefully across his forehead. "Tonight they'll put him someplace else."

"Well, if we can," the guard said.

Shelby was watching him in the mirror: the gray-looking man in the gray guard uniform, R. E. Baylis, who might have been a town constable or a deputy sheriff twenty years ago. "What's the trouble?" Shelby asked.

"I mean he might have been ordered put there, I don't know."

"Ordered by who?"

"Bob Fisher. I say I don't know for sure."

Shelby turned from the mirror. "Bob don't want any trouble."

"Course not."

"Then why would he want to put Sambo in with my boys?"

"I say, I don't know."

Shelby came toward him now, noticing the activity out in the passageway, the convicts standing around and talking, moving slowly as the guards began to form them into two rows. Shelby put a hand on the guard's shoulder. "Mr. Baylis," he said, "don't worry about it. You don't want to ask Bob Fisher; we'll get Sambo out of there ourselves."

"We don't want nobody hurt or anything."

The guard kept looking at him, but Shelby was finished. As far as he was concerned, it was done. He said to Junior, "Give Soonzy the tobacco. You take the soap and stuff."

"It's my turn to keep the tally."

"Don't give me that look, boy."

Junior dropped his tone. "I lugged a box yesterday."

"All right, you handle the tally, Joe Dean carries the soap and stuff." Shelby paused, as if he was going to say something else, then looked at the guard. "Why don't you have the colored boy empty my throne bucket?"

"It don't matter to me," the guard said.

So he pulled Harold Jackson out of line and told him to get down to No. 14—as Joe Dean, Soonzy, and Junior moved along the double row of convicts in the dim passageway and sold them tobacco and cigarette paper, four kinds of plug and scrap, and little tins of snuff, matches, sugar cubes, stick candy, soap bars, sewing needles and thread, playing cards, red bandana handkerchiefs, shoelaces, and combs. They didn't take money; it would waste too much time and they only had ten minutes to go down the double line of eighty-seven men. Junior put the purchase amount in the tally book and the customer had one week to pay. If he didn't pay in a week, he couldn't buy any more stuff until he did. If he didn't pay in two weeks Junior and Soonzy would get him in a cell alone and hit him a few times or stomp the man's ribs and kidneys. If a customer wanted tequila or mescal, or corn whiskey when they had it, he'd come around to No. 14 after supper, before the doors were shut for the night, and pay a dollar a half-pint, put up in medicine bottles from the sick ward that occupied the second floor of the cell block. Shelby only sold alcohol in the morning to three or four of the convicts who needed it first thing or would never get through the day. What most of them wanted was just a day's worth of tobacco and some paper to roll it in.

When the figure appeared outside the iron lattice Shelby said, "Come on in," and watched the big colored boy's reaction as he entered: his gaze shifting twice to take in the double bunk and the boxes and the throne, knowing right away this was a one-man cell.

"I'm Mr. Shelby."

"I'm Mr. Jackson," Harold said.

Frank Shelby touched his mustache. He smoothed it to the sides once, then let his hand drop to the edge of his bunk. His eyes remained on the impassive dark face that did not move now and was looking directly at him.

"Where you from, Mr. Jackson?"

"From Leavenworth."

32

That was it. Big time con in a desert prison hole. "This place doesn't look like much after the federal pen, uh?"

"I been to some was worse, some better."

"What'd you get sent here for?"

"I killed a man was bothering me."

"You get life?"

"Fifteen years."

"Then you didn't kill a man. You must've killed another colored boy." Shelby waited.

Harold Jackson said nothing. He could wait too.

"I'm right, ain't I?" Shelby said.

"The man said for me to come in here."

"He told you, but it was me said for you to come in."

Harold Jackson waited again. "You saying you the man here?"

"Ask any of them out there," Shelby said. "The guards, anybody."

"You bring me in to tell me about yourself?"

"No, I brought you in to empty my slop bucket."

"Who did it before I come?"

"Anybody I told."

"If you got people willing, you better call one of them." Harold turned and had a hand on the door when Shelby stopped him.

"Hey, Sambo—"

Harold came around enough to look at him. "How'd you know that was my name?"

"Boy, you are sure starting off wrong," Shelby said. "I believe you need to be by yourself a while and think it over."

Harold didn't have anything to say to that. He turned

to the door again and left the man standing there playing with his mustache.

As he fell in at the end of the prisoner line, guard named R. E. Baylis gave him a funny look and came over.

"Where's Shelby's bucket at?"

"I guess it's still in there, captain."

"How come he didn't have you take it?"

Harold Jackson stood at attention, looking past the man's face to the stone wall of the passageway. "You'll have to ask him about that, captain."

"Here they come," Bob Fisher said. "Look over there."

Mr. Manly moved quickly from the side of the desk to the window to watch the double file of convicts coming this way. He was anxious to see everything this morning, especially the convicts.

"Is that all of them?"

"In the main cell block. About ninety."

"I thought there'd be more." Mr. Manly studied the double file closely but wasn't able to single out Harold Jackson. All the convicts looked alike. No, that was wrong; they didn't all look alike.

"Since we're shutting down we haven't been getting as many."

"They're all different, aren't they?"

"How's that?" Bob Fisher said.

Mr. Manly didn't answer, or didn't hear him. He stood at the window of the superintendent's office—the largest of a row of offices over the mess hall—and watched the convicts as they came across the yard, passed beyond the end of a low adobe, and came into view again almost directly below the window. The line reached the door of the mess hall and came to a stop.

Their uniforms looked the same, all of them wearing prison stripes, all faded gray and white. It was the hats that were different, light-colored felt hats and a few straw hats, almost identical hats, but all worn at a different angle: straight, low over the eyes, to the side, cocked like a dandy would wear his hat, the brim funneled, the brim up in front, the brim down all around. The hats were as different as the men must be different. He should make a note of that. See if anything had been written on the subject: determining a man's character by the way he wore his hat. But there wasn't a note pad or any paper on the desk and he didn't want to ask Fisher for it right at the moment.

He was looking down at all the hats. He couldn't see any of their faces clearly, and wouldn't unless a man looked up. Nobody was looking up.

They were all looking back toward the yard. Most of them turning now so they wouldn't have to strain their necks. All those men suddenly interested in something and turning to look.

"The women convicts," Bob Fisher said.

Mr. Manly saw them then. My God—two women.

Fisher pressed closer to him at the window. Mr. Manly could smell tobacco on the man's breath. "They just come out of the latrine, that adobe there," Fisher said. "Now watch them boys eyeing them."

The two women walked down the line of convicts, keeping about ten feet away, seeming at ease and not in any hurry, but not looking at the men either.

"Taking their time and giving the boys sweet hell, aren't they? Don't hear a sound, they're so busy licking their lips."

Mr. Manly glanced quickly at the convicts. The way they were looking, it was more likely their mouths were hanging open. It gave him a funny feeling, the men dead serious and no one making a sound.

"My," Fisher said, "how they'd like to reach out and grab a handful of what them girls have got."

"Women—" Mr. Manly said almost as a question. Nobody had told him there were women at Yuma.

A light-brown-haired one and a dark-haired one that looked to be Mexican. Lord God, two good-looking women walking past those men like they were strolling in the park. Mr. Manly couldn't believe they were convicts. They were *women*. The little dark-haired one wore a striped dress—smaller stripes than the men's outfits— that could be a dress she'd bought anywhere. The brown-haired one, taller and a little older, though she couldn't be thirty yet, wore a striped blouse with the top buttons undone, a white canvas belt and a gray skirt that clung to the movement of her hips as she walked and flared out as it reached to her ankles.

"Tacha Reyes," Fisher said

"Pardon me?"

"The little chilipicker. She's been here six months of a ten-year sentence. I doubt she'll serve it all though. She behaves herself pretty good."

36

"What did she do? I mean to be here."

"Killed a man with a knife, she claimed was trying to make her do dirty things."

"Did the other one—kill somebody?"

"Norma Davis? Hell, no. Norma likes to do dirty things. She was a whore till she took up armed robbery and got caught holding up the Citizens' Bank of Prescott, Arizona. Man with her, her partner, was shot dead."

"A woman," Mr. Manly said. "I can't believe a woman would do that."

"With a Colt forty-four," Fisher said. "She shot a policeman during the hold-up but didn't kill him. Listen, you want to keep a pretty picture of women in your head don't get close to Norma. She's serving ten years for armed robbery and attempted murder."

The women were inside the mess hall now. Mr. Manly wanted to ask more questions about them, but he was afraid of sounding too interested and Fisher might get the wrong idea. "I notice some of the men are carrying buckets," he said.

"The latrine detail." Fisher pointed to the low adobe. "They'll go in there and empty them. That's the toilet and wash house, everything sewered clear out to the river. There—now the men are going into mess. They got fifteen minutes to eat, then ten minutes to go to the toilet before the work details form out in the exercise yard."

"Do you give them exercises to do?"

"We give them enough work they don't need any exercise," Fisher answered.

Mr. Manly raised his eyes to look out at the empty yard and was surprised to see a lone convict coming across from the cellblock.

"Why isn't that one with the others?"

Bob Fisher didn't answer right way. Finally he said, "That's Frank Shelby."

"Is he a trusty?"

"Not exactly. He's got some special jobs he does around here."

Mr. Manly let it go. There were too many other things he wanted to know about. Like all the adobe buildings scattered around, a whole row of them over to the left, at the far end of the mess hall. He wondered where the women lived, but didn't ask that.

Well, there was the cook shack over there and the tailor shop, where they made the uniforms. Bob Fisher pointed out the small one-story adobes. Some equipment sheds, a storehouse, the reception hut they were in last night. The mattress factory and the wagon works had been shut down six months ago. Over the main cellblock was the hospital, but the doctor had gone to Florence to set up a sick ward at the new prison. Anybody broke a leg now or crushed his hand working the rocks, they sent for a town doctor.

And the chaplain, Mr. Manly asked casually. Was he still here?

No, there wasn't any chaplain. The last one retired and they decided to wait till after the move to get another. There wasn't many of the convicts prayed anyway.

How would you know that? Mr. Manly wanted to

ask him. But he said, "What are those doors way down there?"

At the far end of the yard he could make out several iron-grill doors, black oval shapes, doorways carved into the solid rock. The doors didn't lead outside, he could tell that, because the top of the east wall and two of the guard towers were still a good piece beyond.

"Starting over back of the main cellblock, you can't see it from here," Bob Fisher said, "a gate leads into the TB cellblock and exercise yard."

"You've got consumptives here?"

"Like any place else. I believe four right now." Fisher hurried on before Mr. Manly could interrupt again. "The doors you can see—one's the crazy hole. Anybody gets mean loco they go in there till they calm down. The next one they call the snake den's a punishment cell."

"Why is it called—"

"I don't know, I guess a snake come in through the air shaft one time. The last door there on the right goes into the women's cellblock. You seen them. We just got the two right now."

There, he could ask about them again and it would sound natural. "The one you said, Norma something, has she been here long?"

"Norma Davis. I believe about a year and a half."

"Do the men ever—I mean I guess you have to sort of watch over the women."

"Mister, we have to watch over everybody."

"But being women—don't they have to have their own, you know, facilities and bath?"

Fisher looked right at Mr. Manly now. "They take a bath in the cook shack three, four times a week."

"In the cook shack." Mr. Manly nodded, surprised. "After the cooks are gone, of course."

"At night," Fisher said. He studied Mr. Manly's profile—the soft pinkish face and gold-frame glasses pressed close to the windowpane—little Bible teacher looking out over his prison and still thinking about Norma Davis, asking harmless sounding questions about the women.

Fisher said quietly, "You want to see them?"

Mr. Manly straightened, looking at Fisher now with a startled expression. "What do you mean?"

"I wondered if you wanted to go downstairs and have another look at Norma and Tacha."

"I want to see everything," Mr. Manly said. "Everything you have here to show me."

3

———◆———

When Frank Shelby entered the mess hall he stepped in line ahead of Junior. In front of him, Soonzy and Joe Dean looked around.

"You take care of it?" Junior asked him.

"He needs some time in the snake den," Shelby said.

Soonzy was looking back down the line. "Where's he at?"

"Last one coming in."

"I'll handle him," Junior said.

Shelby shook his head. "I want somebody else to start it. You and Soonzy break it up and get in some licks."

"No problem," Junior said. "The spook's already got leg-irons on."

They picked up tin plates and cups and passed in front of the serving tables for their beans, salt-dried beef, bread, and coffee. Soonzy and Joe Dean waited, letting Shelby go ahead of them. He paused a moment, holding his food, looking out over the long twelve-man tables and benches that were not yet half filled. Joe Dean moved up next to him. "I see plenty of people that owe us money."

"No, I see the one I want. The Indin," Shelby said, and started for his table.

Raymond San Carlos was pushing his spoon into the beans that were pretty good but would be a lot better with some ketchup. He looked up as Frank Shelby and Junior put their plates down across from him. He hurried and took the spoonful of beans, then took another one more slowly. He knew they had picked him for something. He was sure of it when Soonzy sat down on one side of him and Joe Dean stepped in on the other. Joe Dean acted surprised at seeing him. "Well, Raymond San Carlos," he said, "how are you today?"

"I'm pretty good, I guess."

Junior said, "What're you pretty good at, Raymond?"

"I don't know—some things, I guess."

"You fight pretty good?"

It's coming, Raymond said to himself, and told himself to be very calm and not look away from this little boy son-of-a-bitch friend of Frank Shelby's. He said, "I fight sometimes. Why, you want to fight me?"

"Jesus," Junior said. "Listen to him."

Raymond smiled. "I thought that's what you meant." He picked up his coffee and took a sip.

"Don't drink it," Shelby said.

Raymond looked directly at him for the first time. "My coffee?"

"You see that colored boy? He's picking up his plate." As Raymond looked over Shelby said, "After he sits down I want you to go over and dump your coffee right on his woolly head."

He was at the serving table now, big shoulders and narrow hips. Some of the others from the latrine had come in behind him. He was not the biggest man in the line, but he was the tallest and seemed to have the longest arms.

"You want me to fight him?"

"I said I want you to pour your coffee on his head," Shelby answered. "That's all I said to do. You understand that, or you want me to tell you in sign language?"

Harold Jackson took a place at the end of a table. There were two men at the other end. Shifting his gaze past them as he took a bite of bread, he could see Frank Shelby and the mouthy kid and, opposite them, the big one you would have to hit with a pipe or a pick handle to knock down, and the skinny one, Joe Dean, with the beard that looked like ass fur off a sick dog. The dark-skinned man with them, who was getting up now, he hadn't seen before.

There were five guards in the room. No windows. One door. A stairway—at the end of the room behind the serving tables—where the turnkey and the little man from the train were coming down the stairs now: little man who said he was going to be in charge, looking all around—my, what a fine big mess hall—looking and following the turnkey, who never changed his face, looking at the grub now, nodding, smiling—yes, that would sure stick to their ribs—taking a cup of coffee the turnkey offered him and tasting it. Two of the guards walked over and now the little man was shaking hands with them.

That was when Harold felt somebody behind him brush him, and the hot coffee hitting his head was like a

43

shock, coming into his eyes and feeling as if it was all over him.

Behind him, Raymond said, "What'd you hit my arm for?"

Harold wiped a hand down over his face, twisting around and looking up to see the dark-skinned man who had been with Shelby, an Indian-looking man standing, waiting for him. He knew Shelby was watching, Shelby and anybody else who had seen it happen.

"What's the matter with you?" Harold said.

Raymond didn't move. "I want to know why you hit my arm."

"I'll hit your mouth, boy, you want. But I ain't going to do it here."

Raymond let him have the tin plate, backhanding the edge of it across his eyes, and Harold was off the bench, grabbing Raymond's wrist as Raymond hit him in the face with the coffee cup. Harold didn't get to swing. A fist cracked against his cheekbone from the blind side. He was hit again on the other side of the face, kicked in the small of the back, and grabbed by both arms and around his neck and arched backward until he was looking at the ceiling. There were faces looking at him, the dark-skinned boy looking at him calmly, people pressing in close, then a guard's hat and another, and the turnkey's face with the mustache and the expression that didn't change.

"Like he went crazy," Junior said. "Just reared up and hit this boy."

"I was going past," Raymond said.

Junior was nodding. "That's right. Frank seen it first,

we look over and this spook has got Raymond by the neck. Frank says help him, and me and Soonzy grabbed the spook quick as we could."

The turnkey reached out, but Harold didn't feel his hand. He was looking past him.

"Let him up," Fisher said.

Somebody kicked him again as they jerked him to his feet and let go of his arms. Harold felt his nose throbbing and felt something wet in his eyes. When he wiped at his eyes he saw the red blood on his fingers and could feel it running down his face now. The turnkey's face was raised; he was looking off somewhere.

Fisher said, "You saw it, Frank?"

Shelby was still sitting at his table. He nodded slowly. "Same as Junior told you. That colored boy started it. Raymond hit him to get free, but he wouldn't let go till Junior and Soonzy got over there and pinned him."

"That's all?"

"That's all," Shelby said.

"Anybody else see it start?" Fisher looked around. The convicts met his gaze as it passed over them. They waited as Fisher took his time, letting the silence in the room lengthen. When he looked at Harold Jackson again there was a moment when he seemed about to say something to him. The moment passed. He turned away and walked back to the food tables where Mr. Manly was waiting, his hands folded in front of him, his eyes wide open behind the gold-frame glasses.

"You want to see the snake den," Bob Fisher said. "Come on, we got somebody else wants to see it too."

* * *

After breakfast, as the work details were forming in the yard, the turnkey and the new superintendent and two guards marched Harold Jackson past the groups all the way to the snake den at the back of the yard.

Raymond San Carlos looked at the colored boy as he went by. He had never seen him before this morning. Nobody would see him now for about a week. It didn't matter. Dumb nigger had done something to Shelby and would have to learn, that's all.

While Raymond was still watching them—going one at a time into the cell now—one of the guards, R. E. Baylis, pulled him out of the stone quarry gang and took him over to another detail. Raymond couldn't figure it out until he saw Shelby in the group and knew Shelby had arranged it. A reward for pouring coffee on a man. He was out of that man-breaking quarry and on Shelby's detail because he'd done what he was told. Why not?

As a guard with a Winchester marched them out the main gate Raymond was thinking: Why not do it the easy way? Maybe things were going to be better and this was the beginning of it: get in with Shelby, work for him; have all the cigarettes he wanted, some tequila at night to put him to sleep, no hard-labor details. He could be out of here maybe in twenty years if he never did nothing to wear leg-irons or get put in the snake den. Twenty years, he would be almost fifty years old. He couldn't change that. Or he could do whatever he felt like doing and not smile at people like Frank Shelby and Junior and the two convicts in his cell. He could get his head pounded against the stone wall and spend the rest of his life here. It was a lot to think about, but it made the most sense to get in with Shelby. He would be as dumb as the nigger if he didn't.

Outside the walls, the eight-man detail was marched past the water cistern—their gaze going up the mound of earth past the stonework to the guard tower that looked like a bandstand sitting up there, a nice shady pavilion where a rapid-fire weapon was trained on the main gate—then down the grade to a path that took them along the bluff overlooking the river. They followed it until they reached the cemetery.

Beyond the rows of headstones an adobe wall, low, and uneven, under construction, stood two to three feet high on the riverside of the cemetery.

Junior said, "What do they want a wall for? Them boys don't have to be kept in."

"They want a wall," Shelby said, "because it's a good place for a wall and there ain't nothing else for us to do."

Raymond agreed four year's worth to that. The work was to keep them busy. Everybody knew they would be moving out of here soon, but every day they pounded rocks into gravel for the roads and made adobe bricks and built and repaired walls and levees and cleared brush along the riverbank. It was a wide river with a current—down the slope and across the flat stretch of mud beach to the water—maybe a hundred yards across. There was nothing on the other side—no houses, only a low bank and what looked to be heavy brush. The land over there could be a swamp or a desert; nobody had ever said what it was like, only that it was California.

All morning they laid the big adobe bricks in place, gradually raising the level string higher as they worked

47

on a section of wall at a time. It was dirty, muddy work, and hot out in the open. Raymond couldn't figure out why Shelby was on this detail, unless he felt he needed sunshine and exercise. He laid about half as many bricks as anybody else, and didn't talk to anybody except his three friends. It surprised Raymond when Shelby began working on the other side of the wall from him and told him he had done all right in the mess hall this morning. Raymond nodded; he didn't know what to say. A few minutes went by before Shelby spoke again.

"You want to join us?"

Raymond looked at him. "You mean work for you?"

"I mean go with us," Shelby said. He tapped a brick in place with the handle of his trowel and sliced off the mortar oozing out from under the brick. "Don't look around. Say yes or no."

"I don't know where you're going."

"I know you don't. You say yes or no before I tell you."

"All right," Raymond said. "Yes."

"Can you swim?"

"You mean the river?"

"It's the only thing I see around here to swim," Shelby said. "I'm not going to explain it all now."

"I don't know—"

"Yes, you do, Raymond. You're going to run for the river when I tell you. You're going to swim straight across and find a boat hidden in the brush, put there for us, and you're going to row back fast as you can and meet us swimming over."

"If we're all swimming what do you want the boat for?"

"In case anybody can't make it all the way."

"I'm not sure I can, even."

"You're going to find out," Shelby said.

"How wide is it here?"

"Three hundred fifty feet. That's not so far."

The river had looked cool and inviting before; not to swim across, but to sit in and splash around and get clean after sweating all morning in the adobe mud.

"There's a current—"

"Don't think about it. Just swim."

"But the guard—what about him?"

"We'll take care of the guard."

"I don't understand how we going to do it." He was frowning in the sunlight trying to figure it out.

"Raymond, I say run, you run. All right?"

"You don't give me any time to think about it."

"That's right," Shelby said. "When I leave here you come over the wall and start working on this side." He got up and moved down the wall about ten or twelve feet to where Soonzy and Junior were working.

Raymond stepped over the three-foot section of wall with his mortar bucket and continued working, facing the guard now who was about thirty feet away, sitting on a rise of ground with the Winchester across his lap and smoking a cigarette. Beyond him, a hundred yards or so up the slope, the prison wall and the guard tower at the northwest corner stood against the sky. The guard up there could be looking this way or he could be looking inside, into the yard of the TB cellblock. Make a run for the river with two guns within range. Maybe three, counting the main tower. There was some brush, though, a little cover before he got to the mud flat. But once they saw him, the whistle would blow and they'd be out here like they came up out of the ground, some of them shooting and some of them getting the boat, wherever the boat was kept. He didn't have to stay with Shelby, he could go up to the high country this spring and live by himself. Maybe through the summer. Then go some place nobody knew him and get work. Maybe Mexico.

Joe Dean came along with a wheelbarrow and scooped mortar into Raymond's bucket. "If we're not worried," Joe Dean said, leaning on the wall, "what're you nervous about?"

Raymond didn't look up at him. He didn't like to look at the man's mouth and tobacco-stained teeth showing in his beard. He didn't like having anything to do with the man. He didn't like having anything to do with Junior or Soonzy either. Or with Frank Shelby when he thought about it honestly and didn't get it mixed up with cigarettes and tequila. But he would work with them and swim the river with them to get out of this place. He said to Joe Dean, "I'm ready any time you are."

Joe Dean squinted up at the sun, then let his gaze come down to the guard. "It won't be long," he said, and moved off with his wheelbarrow.

The way they worked it, Shelby kept his eye on the guard. He waited until the man started looking for the chow wagon that would be coming around the corner from the main gate any time now. He waited until the guard was finally half-turned, looking up the slope, then gave a nod to Junior.

Junior jabbed his trowel into the foot of the man working next to him.

The man let out a scream and the guard was on his feet at once, coming down from the rise.

Shelby waited until the guard was hunched over the man, trying to get a look at the foot. The other convicts were crowding in for a look too and the man was holding his ankle, rocking back and forth and moaning. The guard told him goddamn-it, sit still and let him see it.

Shelby looked over at Raymond San Carlos, who was standing now, the wall in front of him as high as his hips. Shelby nodded and turned to the group around the injured man. As he pushed Joe Dean aside he glanced around again to see the wall empty where Raymond had been standing. "What time is it?" he said.

Joe Dean took out his pocket watch. "Eleven-fifty about."

"Exactly."

"Eleven-fifty-two."

Shelby took the watch from Joe Dean as he leaned in to see the clean tear in the toe of the man's shoe and the blood starting to come out. He waited a moment before moving over next to the wall. The guard was asking what happened and Junior was trying to explain how he'd tripped over the goddamn mortar bucket and, throwing his hand out as he fell, his trowel had hit the man's shoe. His foot, the guard said—you stabbed him.

51

Well, he hadn't meant to, Junior told the guard. Jesus, if he'd meant to, he wouldn't have stabbed him in the foot, would he?

From the wall Shelby watched Raymond moving quickly through the brush clumps and not looking back—very good—not hesitating until he was at the edge of the mud flats, a tiny figure way down there, something striped, hunched over in the bushes and looking around now. Go on, Shelby said, looking at the watch. What're you waiting for? It was eleven fifty-three.

The guard was telling the man to take his shoes off, he wasn't going to do it for him; and goddamn-it, get back and give him some air.

When Shelby looked down the slope again Raymond was in the water knee-deep, sliding into it; in a moment only his head was showing. Like he knew what he was doing, Shelby thought.

Between moans the injured man said Oh God, he believed his toes were cut off. Junior said maybe one or two; no trowel was going to take off all a man's toes, 'less you come down hard with the edge; maybe that would do it.

Twenty yards out. Raymond wasn't too good a swimmer, about average. Well, that was all right. If he was average then the watch would show an average time. He sure seemed to be moving slow though. Swimming was slow work.

When the chow wagon comes, the guard said, we'll take him up in it. Two of you men go with him.

It's coming now, somebody said.

There it was, poking along close to the wall, a driver and a helper on the seat, one of the trusties. The guard stood up and yelled for them to get down here. Shelby took time to watch the injured man as he ground his teeth together and eased his shoe off. He wasn't wearing any socks. His toes were a mess of blood, but at least they all seemed to be there. He was lucky.

Raymond was more than halfway across now. The guard was motioning to the wagon, trying to hurry it. So Shelby watched Raymond: just a speck out there, you'd have to know where to look to find him. Wouldn't that be something if he made it? God Almighty, dumb Indin probably could if he knew what to do once he got across. Or if he had some help waiting. But he'd look for the boat that wasn't there and run off through the brush and see all that empty land stretching nowhere.

Eleven fifty-six. He'd be splashing around out there another minute easy before he reached the bank.

Shelby walked past the group around the injured man and called out to the guard who had gone partway up the slope, "Hey, mister!" When the guard looked around Shelby said, "I think there's somebody out there in the water."

The guard hesitated, but not more than a moment before he got over to the wall. He must have had a trained eye, because he spotted Raymond right away and fired the Winchester in the air. Three times in rapid succession.

Joe Dean looked up as Shelby handed him his pocket watch. "He make it?" Joe Dean asked.

"Just about."

"How many minutes?"

"Figure five anyway, as a good average."

Junior said to Shelby, "What do you think?"

"Well, it's a slow way out of here," Shelby answered. "But least we know how long it takes now and we can think on it."

Mr. Manly jumped in his chair and swiveled around to the window when the whistle went off, a high, shrieking sound that ripped through the stillness of the office and seemed to be coming from directly overhead. The first thing he thought of, immediately, was, *somebody's trying to escape*! His first day here . . .

Only there wasn't a soul outside. No convicts, no guards running across the yard with guns.

Of course—they were all off on work details.

When he pressed close to the window Mr. Manly saw the woman, Norma Davis, standing in the door of the tailor shop. Way down at the end of the mess hall. He knew it was Norma, and not the other one. Standing with her hands on her hips, as if she was listening—Lord, as the awful piercing whistle kept blowing. After a few moments she turned and went inside again. Not too concerned about it.

Maybe it wasn't an escape. Maybe it was something else. Mr. Manly went down the hall and opened the doors, looking into empty offices, some that hadn't been used in months. He turned back and, as he reached the end of the hall and the door leading to the outside stairway, the whistle stopped. He waited, then cautiously opened the door and went outside. He could see the front gate from here: both barred doors closed and the inside and outside guards at their posts. He could call to the inside guard, ask him what was going on.

And what if the man looked up at him on the stairs and said it was the noon dinner whistle? It was just about twelve.

Or what if it was an exercise he was supposed to know about? Or a fire drill. Or anything for that matter that a prison superintendent should be aware of. The guard would tell him, "That's the whistle to stop work for dinner, sir," and not say anything else, but his look would be enough.

Mr. Manly didn't know where else he might go, or where he might find the turnkey. So he went back to his office and continued reading the history file on Harold Jackson.

Born Fort Valley, Georgia, September 11, 1879.

Mr. Manly had already read that part. Field hand. No formal education. Arrested in Georgia and Florida several times for disorderly conduct, resisting arrest, striking an officer of the law. Served eighteen months on a Florida prison farm for assault. Inducted into the army April 22, 1898. Assigned to the 24th Infantry Regiment in Tampa, Florida, June 5. Shipped to Cuba.

He was going to read that part over again about Harold Jackson deserting and being court-martialed.

But Bob Fisher, the turnkey, walked in. He didn't knock, he walked in. He looked at Mr. Manly and nodded, then gazed about the room. "If there's something you don't like about this office, we got some others down the hall.

"Caught one of them trying to swim the river, just about the other side when we spotted him." Fisher stopped as Mr. Manly held up his hand and rose from the desk.

"Not right now," Mr. Manly said. "I'm going to go have my dinner. You can give me a written report this afternoon."

Walking past Fisher wasn't as hard as he thought it would be. Out in the hall Mr. Manly paused and looked back in the office. "I assume you've put the man in the snake den."

Fisher nodded.

"Bring me his file along with your report, Bob." Mr. Manly turned and was gone.

4

Harold Jackson recognized the man in the few moments the door was open and the guards were shoving him inside. As the man turned to brace himself Harold saw his face against the outside sunlight, the dark-skinned face, the one in the mess hall. The door slammed closed and they were in darkness. Harold's eyes were used to it after half a day in here. He could see the man feeling his way along the wall until he was on the other side of the ten-by-ten-foot stone cell. It had been almost pitch dark all morning. Now, at midday, a faint light came through the air hole that was about as big around as a stovepipe and tunneled down through the domed ceiling. He could see the man's legs good, then part of his body as he sat down on the bare dirt floor. Harold drew up his legs and stretched them out again so the leg-iron chains would clink and rattle—in case the man didn't know he was here.

Raymond knew. Coming in, he had seen the figure sitting against the wall and had seen his eyes open and close as the sunlight hit his face, black against blackness, a striped animal in his burrow hole. Raymond knew. He had hit the man a good lick across the eyes with his tin plate, and if the man wanted to do something about it, now it was up to him. Raymond would wait, ready for him—while he pictured again Frank Shelby standing by the wall and tried to read Shelby's face.

The guards had brought him back in the skiff, making him row with his arms dead-tired, and dragged him wet and muddy all the way up the hill to the cemetery. Frank Shelby was still there. All of them were, and a man sitting on the ground, his foot bloody. Raymond had wanted to tell Shelby there wasn't any boat over there, and he wanted Shelby to tell him, somehow, what had gone wrong. He remembered Shelby staring at him, but not saying anything with his eyes or his expression. Just staring. Maybe he wasn't picturing Shelby's face clearly now, or maybe he had missed a certain look or gesture from him. He would have time to think about it. Thirty days in here. No mattress, no blanket, no slop bucket, use the corner, or piss on the nigger if he tried something. If the nigger hadn't done something to Shelby he wouldn't be here and you wouldn't be here, Raymond thought. Bread and water for thirty days, but they would take the nigger out before that and he would be alone. There were men they took from here to the crazy hole after being alone in the darkness too long. It can happen if you think about being here and nothing else, Raymond said to himself. So don't think about it. Go over and hit the nigger hard in the face and get it over with. God, if he wasn't so tired.

Kick him in the face to start, Harold was thinking, as he picked at the dried blood crusted on the bridge of his nose. Two and a half steps and aim it for his cheekbone, either side. That would be the way, if he didn't have on the irons and eighteen inches of chain links. He try kicking the man, he'd land flat on his back and the man would be on top of him. He try sneaking up, the man would hear the chain. 'Less the man was asleep and he worked over and got the chain around the man's neck and crossed his legs and stretched and kicked hard. Then they come in and say what happen? And he say I don't know, captain, the man must have choked on his bread. They say yeah, bread can kill a man all right; you stay in here with the bread the rest of your life. So the best thing would be to stand up and let the man stand up and hit him straightaway and beat him enough but not too much. Beat him just right.

He said, "Hey, boy, you ready?"

"Any time," Raymond answered.

"Get up then."

Raymond moved stiffly, bringing up his knees to rise.

"What's the matter with you?"

"I'll tell you something," Raymond said. "If you're any good, maybe you won't get beat too bad. But after I sleep and rest my arms and legs I'll break your jaw."

"What's the matters with your arms and legs?"

"From swimming the river."

Harold Jackson stared at him, interested. He hadn't thought of why the man had been put in here. Now he remembered the whistle. "You saying you tried to bust out?"

"I got across."

"How many of you?"

Raymond hesitated. "I went alone."

"And they over there waiting."

"Nobody was waiting. They come in a boat."

"Broad daylight—man, you must be one dumb Indin fella."

Raymond's legs cramped as he started to rise, and he had to ease down again, slowly.

"We got time," Harold Jackson said. "Don't be in a hurry to get yourself injured."

"Tomorrow," Raymond said, "when the sun's over the hole and I can see your black nigger face in here."

Harold saw the chain around the man's neck and his legs straining to pull it tight. "Indin, you're going to need plenty medicine before I'm through with you."

"The only thing I'm worried about is catching you," Raymond said. "I hear a nigger would rather run than fight."

"Any running I do, red brother, is going to be right at your head."

"I got to see that."

"Keep your eyes open, Indin. You won't see nothing once I get to you."

There was a silence before Raymond said, "I'll tell you something. It don't matter, but I want you to know it anyway. I'm no Indian. I'm Mexican born in the United States, in the territory of Arizona."

"Yeah," Harold Jackson said. "Well, I'm Filipina born in Fort Valley, Georgia."

"Field nigger is what you are."

"Digger Indin talking, eats rats and weed roots."

"I got to listen to a goddamn field hand."

"I've worked some fields," Harold said. "I've plowed and picked cotton, I've skinned mules and dug privies and I've busted rock. But I ain't never followed behind another convict and emptied his bucket for him. White or black. *Nobody.*"

Raymond's tone was lower. "You saw me carrying a bucket this morning?"

"Man, I don't have to see you, I know you carry one every morning. Frank Shelby says dive into it, you dive."

"Who says I work for Frank Shelby?"

"He say scratch my ass, you scratch it. He say go pour your coffee on that nigger's head, you jump up and do it. Man, if I'm a field nigger you ain't no better than a house nigger." Harold Jackson laughed out loud. "Red nigger, that's all you are, boy. A different color but the same thing."

The pain in Raymond's thighs couldn't hold him this time. He lunged for the dark figure across the cell to drive into him and slam his black skull against the wall. But he went in high. Harold got under him and dumped him and rolled to his feet. They met in the middle of the cell, in the dim shaft of light from the air hole, and beat each other with fists until they grappled and kneed and strained against each other and finally went down.

When the guard came in with their bread and water, they were fighting on the hard-packed floor. He yelled to another guard who came fast with a wheelbarrow, pushing it through the door and the short passageway into the cell. They shoveled sand at Harold and Raymond, throwing it stinging hard into their faces until they broke apart and lay gasping on the floor. A little while later another guard came in with irons and chained them to ring bolts on opposite sides of the cell. The door slammed closed and again they were in darkness.

Bob Fisher came through the main gate at eight-fifteen that evening, not letting on he was in a hurry as he crossed the lighted area toward the convicts' mess hall.

He'd wanted to get back by eight—about the time they'd be bringing the two women out of their cellblock and over to the cook shack. But his wife had started in again about staying here and not wanting to move to Florence. She said after sixteen years in this house it was their *home*. She said a rolling stone gathered no moss, and that it wasn't good to be moving all the time. He reminded her they had moved twice in twenty-seven years, counting the move from Missouri. She said then it was about time they settled; a family should stay put, once it planted roots. What family? he asked her. Me and you? His wife said she didn't know anybody in Florence and wasn't sure she wanted to. She didn't even know if there was a Baptist church in Florence. What if there wasn't? What was she supposed to do then? Bob Fisher said that maybe she would keep her fat ass home for a change and do some cooking and baking, instead of sitting with them other fatties all day making patchwork quilts and bad-mouthing everybody in town who wasn't a paid-up member of the church. He didn't honestly care where she spent her time, or whether she baked pies and cakes or not. It was something to throw at her when she started in nagging about staying in Yuma. She said how could anybody cook for a person who came home at all hours with whiskey stinking up his breath? Yes, he had stopped and had a drink at the railroad hotel, because he'd had to talk to the express agent about moving equipment to Florence. Florence, his wife said. She wished she had never heard the name—the same name as her cousin who was still living in Sedalia, but now she didn't even like to think of her cousin any more and they had grown up together as little girls. Bob Fisher couldn't picture his wife as a little girl. No, that tub of fat couldn't have ever been a little girl. He didn't tell her that. He told her he had to get back to the prison, and left without finishing his coffee.

Fisher walked past the outside stairway and turned the corner of the mess hall. There were lights across the way in the main cellblock. He moved out into the yard enough to look up at the second floor of the mess hall and saw a light on in the superintendent's office. The little Sunday school teacher was still there, or had come back after supper. Before going home Fisher had brought in his written report of the escape and the file on Raymond San Carlos. The Sunday school teacher had been putting his books away, taking them out of a suitcase and lining them up evenly on the shelf. He'd said just lay the report on the desk and turned back to his books. What would he be doing now? Probably reading his Bible.

Past the latrine adobe Fisher walked over to the mess hall and tried the door. Locked for the night. Now he moved down the length of the building, keeping close to the shadowed wall though moving at a leisurely pace— just out for a stroll, checking around, if anybody was curious. At the end of the building he stopped and looked both ways before crossing over into the narrow darkness between the cook-shack adobe and the tailor shop.

Now all he had to do was find the right brick to get a free show. About chin-high it was, on the right side of the cook-shack chimney that stuck out from the wall about a foot and would partly hide him as he pressed in close. Fisher worked a finger in on both sides of the brick that had been chipped loose some months before, and pulled it out as slowly as he could. He didn't look inside right away; no, he always put the brick on the ground first and set himself, his feet wide apart and his shoulders hunched a little so the opening would be exactly at eye level. They would be just past the black iron range, this side of the work table where they always placed the washtub, with the bare electric light on right above them.

Fisher looked in. Goddamn Almighty, just in time.

Just as Norma Davis was taking off her striped shirt, already unbuttoned, slipping it off her shoulders to let loose those round white ninnies that were like nothing he had ever seen before. Beauties, and she knew it, too, the way she stuck them out, standing with her hands on her hips and her belly a round little mound curving down into her skirt. What was she waiting for? Come on, Fisher said, take the skirt off and get in the tub. He didn't like it when they only washed from the waist up. With all the rock dust in the air and bugs from the mattresses and sweating under those heavy skirts, a lick-and-a-promise, armpits-and-neck wash wasn't any good. They had to wash theirselves all over to be clean and healthy.

Maybe he could write it into the regulations: Women convicts must take a full bath every other day. Or maybe every day.

The Mexican girl, Tacha Reyes, appeared from the left, coming from the end of the stove with a big pan of steaming water, and poured it into the washtub. Tacha was still dressed. Fisher could tell by her hair she hadn't bathed yet. She had to wait on Norma first, looking at Norma now as she felt the water. Tacha had a nice face; she was just a little skinny. Maybe give her more to eat—

Norma was taking off her skirt. Yes, *sir,* and that was all she had. No underwear on. Bare-ass naked with black stockings that come up over her knees. Norma turned, leaning against the work table to pull the stockings off, and Bob Fisher was looking at the whole show. He watched her lay her stockings on the table. He watched her pull her hair back with both hands and look down at her ninnies as she twisted the hair around so it would stay. He watched her step over to the tub, scratching under one of her arms, and say, "If it's too hot I'll put you in it."

"It should be all right," Tacha said.

Another voice, not in the room but out behind him, a voice he knew, said, "Guard, what's the matter? Are you sick?"

Twisting around, Bob Fisher hit the peak of his hat on the chimney edge and was straightening it, his back to the wall, as Mr. Manly came into the space between the buildings.

"It's me," Fisher said.

"Oh, I didn't know who it was."

"Making the rounds. I generally check all the buildings before I go to bed."

Mr. Manly nodded. "I thought somebody was sick, the way you were leaning against the wall."

"No, I feel fine. Hardly ever been sick."

"It was the way you were standing, like you were throwing up."

"No, I was just taking a look in here. Dark places you got to check good." He couldn't see Mr. Manly's eyes, but he knew the little son of a bitch was looking right at him, staring at him, or past him, where part of the brick opening might be showing and he could see light coming through. "You ready to go," Fisher said, "I'll walk you over to the gate."

He came out from the wall to close in on Mr. Manly and block his view; but he was too late.

"What's that hole?" Mr. Manly said.

"A hole?"

"Behind you, I can see something—"

Bob Fisher turned to look at the opening, then at Mr. Manly again. "Keep your voice down."

"Why? What is it?"

"I wasn't going to say anything. I mean it's something I generally check on myself. But," Fisher said, "if you want to take a look, help yourself."

Mr. Manly frowned. He felt funny now standing here in the darkness. He said in a hushed tone, "Who's in there?"

"Go ahead, take a look."

Through the slit of the opening something moved, somebody in the room. Mr. Manly stepped close to the wall and peered in.

The light glinted momentarily on his glasses as his head came around, his eyes wide open.

"She doesn't have any clothes on!"

"Shhhh." Fisher pressed a finger to his heavy mustache. "Look and see what they're doing."

"She's bare-naked, washing herself."

"We want to be sure that's all," Fisher said.

"What?"

"Go on, see what she's doing."

Mr. Manly leaned against the wall, showing he was calm and not in any hurry. He peered in again, as though looking around a corner. Gradually his head turned until his full face was pressed against the opening.

What Norma was doing, she was sliding a bar of yellow soap over her belly and down her thighs, moving her legs apart, and coming back up with the soap almost to her breasts before she slid it down again in a slow circular motion. Mr. Manly couldn't take his eyes off her. He watched the Mexican girl bring a kettle and pour water over Norma's shoulders, and watched the suds run down between her breasts, Lord Jesus, through the valley and over the fertile plain and to the dark forest. He could feel his heart beating and feel Bob Fisher close behind him. He had to quit looking now; Lord, it was long enough. It was too long. He wanted to clear his throat. She was turning around and he got a glimpse of her behind as he pulled his face from the opening and stepped away.

"Washing herself," Mr. Manly said. "That's all I could see she was doing."

Bob Fisher nodded. "I hoped that was all." He stooped to pick up the brick and paused with it at the opening. "You want to look at Tacha?"

"I think I've seen enough to know what they're doing," Mr. Manly answered. He walked out to the open yard and waited there for Fisher to replace the brick and follow him out.

"What I want to know is what you're doing spying on them."

"Spying? I was checking, like I told you, to see they're not doing anything wrong."

"What do you mean, wrong?"

"Anything that ain't natural, then. You know what I mean. Two women together without any clothes on—I want to know there ain't any funny business going on."

"She was washing herself."

"Yes, sir," Fisher said, "that's all I saw too. The thing is, you never know when they might start."

Mr. Manly could still see her, the bar of yellow soap moving over her body. "I've never heard of anything like that. They're both *women*."

"I'll agree with you there," Fisher said, "but in a prison you never know. We got men with no women, and women with no men, and I'll tell you we got to keep our eyes open if we don't want any funny business."

"I've heard tell of men," Mr. Manly said—the sudsy water running down between her breasts—"but *women*. What do you suppose they do?"

"I hope I never find out," Fisher said. He meant it, too.

He got Mr. Manly out of there before the women came out and saw them standing in the yard; he walked Mr. Manly over to the main gate and asked him if he had read the report on the escape attempt.

Mr. Manly said yes, and that he thought it showed the guards to be very alert. He wondered, though, wasn't this Raymond San Carlos the same one the Negro has assaulted in the mess hall? The very same, Fisher said. Then wasn't it dangerous to put them both in the same cell? Dangerous to who? Fisher asked. To *them*, they were liable to start fighting again and try and kill each other. They already tried, Fisher said. They were chained to the floor now out of each other's reach. Mr. Manly asked how long they would leave them like that, and Fisher said until they made up their minds to be good and kind to each other. Mr. Manly said that could be never if there was a grudge between them. Fisher said it didn't matter to him, it was up to the two boys.

Fisher waited in the lighted area as Mr. Manly passed through the double gates of the sally port and walked off toward the superintendent's cottage. He was pretty sure Mr. Manly had believed his story, that he was checking on the women to see they didn't do queer things. He'd also bet a dollar the little Sunday school teacher wouldn't make him chink the hole up either.

That was dumb, taking all his books over to the office. Mr. Manly sat in the living room of the superintendent's cottage, in his robe and slippers, and didn't have a thing to read. His Bible was on the night table in the bedroom. Yes, and he'd made a note to look up what St. Paul said about being in prison, something about all he'd gone through and how one had to have perseverance. He saw Norma Davis rubbing the bar of soap over her body, sliding it up and down. No—what he wished he'd brought were the file records of the two boys in the snake den. He would have to talk to them when they got out. Say to them, look, boys, fighting never solved anything. Now forget your differences and shake hands.

They were different all right, a Negro and an Indian. But they were alike too.

Both here for murder. Both born the same year. Both had served time. Both had sketchy backgrounds and no living relatives anybody knew of. The deserter and the deserted.

A man raised on a share-crop farm in Georgia; joined the army and, four months later, was listed as a deserter. Court-martialed, sentenced to hard labor.

A man raised on the San Carlos Indian reservation; deserted by his Apache renegade father before he was born. Father believed killed in Mexico; mother's whereabouts unknown.

Both of them in the snake den now, a little room carved out of stone, with no light and hardly any air. Waiting to get at each other.

Maybe the sooner he talked to them the better. Bring them both out in ten days—no matter what Bob Fisher thought about it. Ten days was long enough. They needed spiritual guidance as much as they needed corporal punishment. He'd tell Fisher in the morning.

As soon as Mr. Manly got into bed he started thinking of Norma Davis again, seeing her clearly with the bare light right over her and her body gleaming with soap and water. He saw her in the room then, her body still slippery-looking in the moonlight that was coming through the window. Before she could reach the bed, Mr. Manly switched on the night-table lamp, grabbed hold of his Bible and leafed as fast as he could to St. Paul's letters to the Corinthians.

For nine days neither of them spoke. They sat facing each other, their leg-irons chained to ring bolts that were cemented in the floor. Harold would stand and stretch and lean against the wall and Raymond would watch him. Later on Raymond would get up for a while and Harold would watch. They never stood up at the same time or looked at each other directly. There was silence except for the sound of the chains when they moved. Each pretended to be alone in the darkness of the cell, though each was intently aware of the other's presence. Every day about noon a guard brought them hardtack and water. The guard was not allowed to speak to them, and neither of them spoke to him. It was funny their not talking, he told the other guards. It was spooky. He had never known a man in the snake den not to talk a storm when he was brought his bread and water. But these two sat there as if they had been hypnotized.

The morning of the tenth day Raymond said, "They going to let you out today." The sound of his voice was strange, like someone else's voice. He wanted to clear his throat, but wouldn't let himself do it with the other man watching him. He said, "Don't go anywhere, because

71

when I get out of here I'm going to come looking for you."

"I be waiting," was all Harold Jackson said.

At midday the sun appeared in the air shaft and gradually faded. Nobody brought their bread and water. They had been hungry for the first few days but were not hungry now. They waited and it was early evening when the guard came in with a hammer and pounded the ring bolts open, both of them, Raymond watching him curiously but not saying anything. Another guard came in with shovels and a bucket of sand and told them to clean up their mess.

Bob Fisher was waiting outside. He watched them come out blinking and squinting in the daylight, both of them filthy stinking dirty, the Negro with a growth of beard and the Indian's bony face hollowed and sick-looking. He watched their gaze creep over the yard toward the main cellblock where the convicts were standing around and sitting by the wall, most of them looking this way.

"You can be good children," Fisher said, "or you can go back in there, I don't care which. I catch you fighting, twenty days. I catch you looking mean, twenty days." He looked directly at Raymond. "I catch you swimming again, thirty days and leg-irons a year. You understand me?"

For supper they had fried mush and syrup, all they wanted. After, they were marched over to the main cellblock. Raymond looked for Frank Shelby in the groups standing around outside, but didn't see him. He saw Junior and nodded. Junior gave him a deadpan look. The guard, R. E. Baylis, told them to get their blankets and any gear they wanted to bring along.

"You putting us in another cell?" Raymond asked him. "How about make it different cells? Ten days, I'll smell him the rest of my life."

"Come on," Baylis said. He marched them down the passageway and through the rear gate of the cellblock.

"Wait a minute," Raymond said. "Where we going?"

The guard looked around at him. "Didn't nobody tell you? You two boys are going to live in the TB yard."

5

A work detail was making adobe bricks over by the south wall, inside the yard. They mixed mud and water and straw, stirred it into a heavy wet paste and poured it into wooden forms. There were bricks drying all along the base of the wall and scrap lumber from the forms and stacks of finished bricks, ready to be used here or sold in town.

Harold Jackson and Raymond San Carlos had to come across the yard with their wheelbarrows to pick up bricks and haul them back to the TB cellblock that was like a prison within a prison: a walled-off area with its own exercise yard. There were eight cells here, in a row facing the yard, half of them empty. The four tubercular convicts stayed in their cells most of the time or sat in the shade and watched Harold and Raymond work, giving them advice and telling them when a line of bricks wasn't straight. They were working on the face wall of the empty cells, tearing out the weathered, crumbling adobe and putting in new bricks; repairing cells that would probably never again be occupied. This was their main job. They worked at it side by side without saying a word to each other. They also had to bring the tubercular convicts their meals, and sometimes get cough medicine from the sick ward. A guard gave them white cotton doctor masks they could put on over their nose and mouth for whenever they went into the TB cells; but the masks were hot and hard to breathe through, so they didn't wear them after the first day. They used the masks, and a few rags they found, to pad the leg-irons where the metal dug into their ankles.

The third day out of the snake den Raymond began talking to the convicts on the brick detail. He recognized Joe Dean in the group, but didn't speak to him directly. He said, man alive, it was good to breathe fresh air again and feel the sun. He took off his hat and looked up at the sky. All the convicts except Joe Dean went on working. Raymond said, even being over with the lungers was better than the snake den. He said somebody must have made a mistake, he was supposed to be in thirty days for trying to escape, but they let him out after ten. Raymond smiled; he said he wasn't going to mention it to them, though.

Joe Dean was watching him, leaning on his shovel. "You take care of him yet?"

"Take care of who?" Raymond asked him.

"The nigger boy. I hear he stomped you."

"Nobody stomped me. Where'd you hear that?"

"Had to chain him up."

"They chained us both."

"Looks like you're partners now," Joe Dean said.

"I'm not partners with him. They make us work together, that's all."

"You going to fight him?"

"Sure, when I get a chance."

"He don't look too anxious," another convict said. "That nigger's a big old boy."

"I got to wait for the right time," Raymond said. "That's all."

He came back later for another wheelbarrow load of bricks and stood watching them as they worked the mud and mixed in straw. Finally he asked if anybody had seen Frank around.

"Frank who you talking about?" Joe Dean asked.

"Frank Shelby."

"Listen to him," Joe Dean said. "He wants to know has anybody seen Frank."

"I got to talk to him," Raymond said. "See if he can get me out of there."

"Scared of TB, huh?"

"I mean being with the black boy. I got enough of him."

"I thought you wanted to fight him."

"I don't know," Joe Dean said. "It sounds to me like you're scared to start it."

"I don't want no more of the snake den. That's the only thing stopping me."

"You want to see Frank Shelby," one of the other convicts said, "there he is." The man nodded and Raymond looked around.

Shelby must have just come out of the mess hall. He stood by the end-gate of a freight wagon that Junior and Soonzy and a couple of other convicts were unloading. There was no guard with them, unless he was inside. Raymond looked up at the guard on the south wall.

"I'll tell you something," Joe Dean said. "You can forget about Frank helping you."

Raymond was watching the guard. "You know, uh? You know him so good he's got you working in this adobe slop."

"Sometimes we take bricks to town," Joe Dean said. "You think on it if you don't understand what I mean."

"I got other things to think on."

As the guard on the south wall turned and started for the tower at the far end of the yard, Raymond picked up his wheelbarrow and headed for the mess hall.

Shelby didn't look up right away. He was studying a bill of lading attached to a clipboard, checking things off. He said to Junior, "The case right by your foot, that should be one of ours."

"Says twenty-four jars of Louisiana cane syrup."

"It's corn whiskey." Shelby still didn't look up, but he said then, "What do you want?"

"They let me out of the snake den," Raymond said. "I was suppose to be in thirty days, they let me out."

Shelby looked at him now. "Yeah?"

"I wondered if you fixed it."

"Not me."

"I thought sure." He waited as Shelby looked in the wagon and at the clipboard again. "Say, what happened at the river? I thought you were going to come right behind me."

"It didn't work out that way."

"Man, I thought I had made it. But I couldn't find no boat over there."

"I guess you didn't look in the right place," Shelby said.

"I looked where you told me. Man, it was work. I don't like swimming so much." He watched Shelby studying the clipboard. "I was wondering—you know I'm over in a TB cell now."

Shelby didn't say anything.

"I was wondering if you could fix it, get me out of there."

"Why?"

"I got to be with that nigger all the time."

"He's got to be with you," Shelby said, "so you're even."

Raymond grinned. "I never thought of it that way." He waited again. "What do you think?"

"About what?"

"About getting me back with everybody."

Shelby started fooling with his mustache, smoothing it with his fingers. "Why do you think anybody wants you back?"

Raymond didn't grin this time. "I did what you told me," he said seriously. "Listen, I'll work for you any time you want."

"I'm not hiring today."

"Well, what about getting me out of the TB yard?"

Shelby looked at him. He said, "Boy, why would I do that? I'm the one had you put there. Now you say one more word Soonzy is going to come down off the wagon and break both your arms."

Shelby watched Raymond pick up his wheelbarrow and walk away. "Goddamn Indin is no better than a nigger," he said to Junior. "You treat them nice one time and you got them hanging around the rest of your life."

When Raymond got back to the brick detail Joe Dean said, "Well, what did he say?"

"He's going to see what he can do," Raymond answered. He didn't feel like talking any more, and was busy loading bricks when Harold Jackson came across the yard with his wheelbarrow. Harold wore his hat pointed low over his eyes. He didn't have a shirt on and, holding the wheelbarrow handles, his shoulders and arm muscles were bunched and hard-looking. One of the convicts saw him first and said to Raymond, "Here comes your buddy." The other convicts working the adobe mud looked up and stood leaning on their shovels and hoes as Harold Jackson approached.

Raymond didn't look at him. He stacked another brick in the wheelbarrow and got set to pick up the handles. He heard one of the convicts say, "This here Indian says you won't fight him. Says you're scared. Is that right?"

"I fight him any time he wants."

Raymond had to look up then. Harold was staring at him.

"Well, I don't know," the convict said. "You and him talk about fighting, but nobody's raised a hand yet."

"It must be they're both scared," Joe Dean said. "Or it's because they're buddies. All alone in that snake den they got to liking each other. Guard comes in thinks they're rassling on the floor—man, they're not fighting, they're buggering each other."

The other convicts grinned and laughed, and one of them said, "Jesus Christ, what they are, they're sweethearts."

Raymond saw Harold Jackson take one step and hit the man in the face as hard as he could. Raymond wanted to say no, don't do it. It was a strange thing and happened quickly as the man spun toward him and Raymond put up his hands. One moment he was going to catch the man, keep him from falling against him. The next moment he balled up a fist and drove it into the man's face, right out in the open yard, the dumbest thing he had ever done, but doing it now and not stopping or thinking, going for Joe Dean now and busting him hard in the mouth as he tried to bring up his shovel. God, it felt good, a wild hot feeling, letting go and stepping into them and swinging hard at all the faces he had been wanting to smash and pound against a wall.

Harold Jackson held back a moment, staring at the crazy Indian, until somebody was coming at him with a shovel and he had to grab the handle and twist and chop it across the man's head. If he could get room and swing the shovel—but there were too many of them too close, seven men in the brick detail and a couple more, Junior and Soonzy, who came running over from the supply detail and grabbed hunks of lumber and started clubbing at the two wild men.

By the time the guard on the south wall fired his Winchester in the air and a guard came running over from the mess hall, Harold lay stunned in the adobe muck; Raymond was sprawled next to him and neither of them moved.

"Lord," Junior said, "we had to take sticks this time to get them apart."

Soonzy shook his head. "I busted mine on that nigger, he went right on fighting."

"They're a scrappy pair," Junior said, "but they sure are dumb, ain't they?"

Bob Fisher told the guard to hose them off and throw them in the snake den. He told Soonzy and Junior and the men on the brick detail to get back to work. Chained? the guard wanted to know. Chained, Fisher said, and walked off toward the stairs at the end of the mess hall, noticing the convicts who had come out of the adobe huts and equipment sheds, brought out by the guard's rifle fire, all of them looking toward the two men lying in the mud. He noticed Frank Shelby and some convicts by the freight wagon. He noticed the cooks in their white aprons, and the two women, Norma and Tacha, over by the tailor shop.

Fisher went up the stairs and down the hall to the superintendent's office. As he walked in, Mr. Manly turned from the window.

"The same two," Fisher said.

"It looked like they were all fighting." Mr. Manly glanced at the window again.

"You want a written report?"

"I'd like to know what happened."

"Those two start fighting. The other boys try to pull

them apart and the two start swinging at everybody. Got to hit 'em with shovels to put 'em down."

"I didn't see them fighting each other."

"Then you must have missed that part." Past Mr. Manly's thoughtful expression—through the window and down in the yard—he saw a convict walking toward the tailor shop with a bundle under his arm. Frank Shelby. This far away he knew it was Shelby. Norma Davis stood in the door waiting for him.

"Soon as I heard the shots," Mr. Manly said, "I looked out. They were separated, like two groups fighting. They didn't look close enough to have been fighting each other."

Bob Fisher waited. "You want a written report?"

"What're you going to do to them?"

"I told them before, they start fighting they go back in the snake den. Twenty days. They know it, so it won't be any surprise."

"Twenty days in there seems like a long time."

"I hope to tell you it is," Fisher said.

"I was going to talk to them when they got out the other day. I meant to—I don't know, I put it off and then I guess some other things came up."

Fisher could see Shelby at the tailor shop now, close to the woman, talking to her. She turned and they both went inside.

"I'm not saying I could have prevented their fighting, but you never know, do you? Maybe if I *had* spoken to them, got them to shake hands—you understand what I mean, Bob?"

Fisher pulled his gaze away from the tailor shop to the little man by the window. "Well, I don't know about that."

"It could have made a difference."

"I never seen talking work much on anybody."

"But twenty days in there," Mr. Manly said, "and it could be my fault, because I didn't talk to them." He paused. "Don't you think, Bob, in this case, you ought to give them no more than ten days? You said yourself ten days was a long time. Then soon as they come out I'll talk to them."

"That Indian was supposed to be in thirty days," Fisher said, "and you changed it to ten. Now I've already told them twenty and you want to cut it down again. I tell a convict one thing and you say something else and we begin to have problems."

"I'm only asking," Mr. Manly said, "because if I could have done something, if I'm the one to blame, then it wouldn't be fair to those two boys."

"Mister, they're convicts. They do what we tell them. Anything."

Mr. Manly agreed, nodding. "That's true, we give the orders and they have to obey. But we still have to be fair, no matter who we're dealing with."

Bob Fisher wondered what the hell he was doing here arguing with this little four-eyed squirt. He said, "They don't know anything about this. They don't know you meant to talk to them."

"But I know it," Mr. Manly said, "and the more I think about it the more I know I got to talk to them." He paused. "Soon."

Fisher saw it coming, happening right before his eyes, the little squirt's mind working behind his gold-frame glasses.

"Yes, maybe you ought to bring them in tomorrow."

"Just a minute ago you said ten days—"

"Do you have any children, Bob?"

The question stopped Fisher. He shook his head slowly, watching Mr. Manly.

"Well, I'm sure you know anyway you got to have patience with children. Sure, you got to punish them sometimes, but first you got to teach them right from wrong and be certain they understand it."

"I guess my wife's got something wrong with her. She never had any kids."

"That's God's will, Bob. What I'm getting at, these two boys here, Harold and Raymond, they're just like children." Mr. Manly held up his hand. "I know what you're going to say, these boys wasn't caught stealing candy, they took a life. And I say that's true. But still they're like little children. They're grown in body but not in mind. They got the appetites and temptations of grown men. They fight and carry on and, Lord knows, they have committed murder, for which they are now paying the price. But we don't want no more murders around here, do we, Bob? No, sir. Nor do we want to punish anybody for something that isn't their fault. We got two murderers wanting to kill each other. Two mean-looking boys we chain up in a dungeon. But Bob, tell me something. Has anybody ever spoke kindly to them? I mean has anybody ever helped them overcome the hold the devil's got on them? Has anybody ever showed them the path of righteousness, or explained to them Almighty God's justice and the meaning of ever-lasting salvation?"

Jesus Christ, Bob Fisher said—not to Mr. Manly, to himself. He had to get out of here; he didn't need any sermons today. He nodded thoughtfully and said to Mr. Manly, "I'll bring them in here whenever you want."

When Junior and Soonzy came back from clubbing the Indian and the colored boy, Frank Shelby told them to get finished with the unloading. He told them to leave a bottle of whiskey in the wagon for the freight driver and take the rest of it to his cell. Soonzy said Jesus, that nigger had a hard head, and showed everybody around how the hunk of wood was splintered. Junior said my, but they were dumb to start a fight out in the yard. This old boy over there called them sweethearts and that had started them swinging. If they wanted to fight, they should have it out in a cell some night. A convict standing there said, boy, he'd like to see that. It would be a good fight.

Shelby was looking at Norma Davis outside the tailor shop. He knew she was waiting for him, but what the convict said caught in his mind and he looked at the man.

"Which one would you bet on?"

"I think I'd have to pick the nigger," the convict said. "The way he's built."

Shelby looked around at Soonzy. "Who'd you pick?"

"I don't think neither of them look like much."

"I said who'd you pick."

"I don't know. I guess the nigger."

"How about in the mess hall," Shelby said. "The Indin showed he's got nerve. Pretty quick, too, the way he laid that plate across the boy's eyes."

"He's quick," Junior said.

"Quick and stronger than he looks," Shelby said. "You saw him swimming against the river current."

"Well, he's big for an Indin," Junior said. "Big and quick and, as Frank says, he's got some nerve. Another thing, you don't see no marks on him from their fighting in the snake den. He might be more'n the nigger can handle."

"I'd say you could bet either way on that fight," Shelby said. He told Junior to hand him the bundle for the tailor shop—a bolt of prison cloth wrapped in brown paper—and walked off with it.

Most of them, Shelby was thinking, would bet on the nigger. Get enough cons to bet on the Indin and it could be a pretty good pot. If he organized the betting, handled the whole thing, he could take about ten percent for the house. Offer some long-shot side bets and cover those himself. First, though, he'd have to present the idea to Bob Fisher. A prize fight. Fisher would ask what for and he'd say two reasons. Entertain the cons and settle the problem of the two boys fighting. Decide a winner and the matter would be ended. Once he worked out the side bets and the odds.

"Bringing me a present?" Norma asked him.

Shelby reached the shade of the building and looked up at her in the doorway. "I got a present for you, but it ain't in this bundle."

"I bet I know what it is."

"I bet you ought to. Who's inside?"

"Just Tacha and the old man."

"Well, you better invite me in," Shelby said, "before I start stripping you right here."

"Little anxious today?"

"I believe it's been over a week."

"Almost two weeks," Norma said. "Is there somebody else?"

"Two times I was on my way here," Shelby said, "Fisher stopped me and sent me on a work detail."

"I thought you got along with him."

"It's the first time he's pulled anything like that."

"You think he knows about us?"

"I imagine he does."

"He watches me and Tacha take a bath."

"He comes in?"

"No, there's a loose brick in the wall he pulls out. One time, after I was through, I peeked out the door and saw him sneaking off."

Shelby grinned. "Dirty old bastard."

"Maybe he doesn't feel so old."

"I bet he'd like to have some at that." Shelby nodded slowly. "I just bet he would."

Norma was watching him. "Now what are you thinking?"

"But he wouldn't want anybody to know about it. That's why he don't come in when you're taking a bath. Tacha's there."

Norma smiled. "I can see your evil mind working. If Tacha wasn't there—"

"Yes, sir, then he'd come in."

"Ask if I wanted him to soap my back."

"Front and back. I can see him," Shelby said. "One thing leads to another. After the first time, he don't soap you. No, sir, he gets right to it."

"Then one night you come in"—Norma giggled—"and catch the head guard molesting a woman convict."

Shelby shook his head, grinning.

"He's trying to pull his pants on in a hurry and you say, Good evening, Mr. Fisher. How are tricks?"

"God *damn*," Shelby said. "that's good."

"He's trying to button his pants and stick his shirt in and thinking as hard as he can for something to say." Norma kept giggling and trying not to. "He says, uh—"

"What does he say?"

"He says, 'I just come in for some coffee. Can I get you a cup, Mr. Shelby?' And you say, 'No, thank you. I was just on my way to see the superintendent.' He says, 'About what, Mr. Shelby?' And you say, 'About how some of the guards have been messing with the women convicts.'"

"It's an idea," Shelby said, "but I don't know of anything he can do for me except open the gate and he ain't going to do that, no matter what I get on him. No, I was wondering—if you and him got to be good friends—what he might tell you if you were to ask him."

Norma raised her arm and used the sleeve to wipe the wetness from her eyes. "What might he tell me?"

"Like what day we're supposed to move out of here. If we're going by train. If we're all going at once, or in groups." Shelby spoke quietly and watched her begin to nod her head as she thought about it. "Once we know when we're moving we can begin to make plans. I can talk to my brother Virgil, when he comes to visit, get him working on the outside. But we got to know *when*."

Norma was picturing herself in the cook shack with Fisher. "It would have to be the way I asked him. So he wouldn't suspect anything."

"Honey, you'd know better than I could tell you."

"I suppose once I got him comfortable with me."

"You won't have any trouble at all."

"It'll probably be a few times before he relaxes."

"Get him to think you like him. A man will believe anything when he's got his pants off."

"We might be having a cup of coffee after and I'll make a little face and look around the kitchen and say, 'Gee, honey, I wish there was some place else we could go.'"

"Ask him about the new prison."

"That's what I'm leading to," Norma said. "I'll tell him I hope we'll have a better place than this. Then I'll say, like I just thought of it, 'By the way, honey, when are we going to this new prison?'"

"Ask him if he's ever done it on a train?"

"I'll think of a way. I bet he's a horny old bastard."

"So much the better. He's probably never got it off a good-looking woman before in his life."

"Thank you."

"You're welcome."

"The only thing is what to do about Tacha."

"I'll have to think on that," Shelby said.

"Maybe he'd like both of us."

"Honey, he don't even have dreams like that anymore."

Tacha Reyes looked up from her sewing machine as they came into the shop and Shelby dropped the bundle on the work table. The old man, who had been a tailor here for twenty-six years since murdering his wife, continued working. He sat hunched over with his legs crossed, sewing a button to a striped convict coat.

Norma didn't say anything to them. She followed Shelby into the back room where the supplies and bolts of material were kept. The first few times they went back there together she said they were going to inventory the material or look over the thread supply or count buttons. Now she didn't bother. They went into the room and closed the door.

Tacha sat quietly, not moving. She told herself she shouldn't listen, but she always did. Sometimes she heard Norma, the faint sound of her laughing in there; she never heard Frank Shelby. He was always quiet.

Like the man who owned the café in St. David. He would come up behind her when she was working in the kitchen and almost before she heard him he would be touching her, putting his hands on her hips and bringing them up under her arms, pretending to be counting her ribs and asking how come she was so skinny, how come, huh, didn't she like the cooking here? And when she twisted away from him—what was the matter, didn't she like working here?

"How can he come in," Tacha said, "do whatever he wants?"

91

The tailor glanced over at the stock-room door. He didn't look at Tacha. "Norma isn't complaining."

"She's as bad as he is."

"I wouldn't know about that."

"She does whatever he wants. But he's a convict, like any of them."

"I'll agree he's a convict," the tailor said.

"You're afraid to even talk about him."

"I'll agree to that too," the tailor said.

"Some people can do whatever they want. Other people have to let them." Tacha was silent again. What good was talking about it?

The owner of the café in St. David thought he could do whatever he wanted because he paid her seven dollars a week and said she didn't have to stay if she didn't want to. He would kiss her and she would have to close her eyes hard and hold her breath and feel his hand coming up over her breast. Her sister had said so what, he touches you a little. Where else are you going to make seven dollars a week? But I don't want him to, Tacha had said. I don't love him. And her sister had told her she was crazy. You don't have to love a man even to marry him. This man was providing for her and she should look at it that way. He gave her something, she should give him something.

She gave him the blade of a butcher knife late one afternoon when no one was in the café and the cook had gone to the outhouse. She jabbed the knife into him because he was hurting her, forcing her back over the kitchen table, smothering her with his weight and not giving her a chance to speak, to tell him she wanted to quit. Her fingers touched the knife on the table and, in that little moment of panic, as his hand went under her skirt and up between her legs, she pushed the knife into his stomach. She would remember his funny, surprised expression and remember him pushing away from her again with his weight, and looking down at the knife handle, touching it gently with both hands then, standing still, as if afraid to move, and looking down at the knife. She remembered saying, "I didn't mean to—" and thinking, Take it out, you can do whatever you want to me, I didn't mean to do this.

"Some people lead," the tailor said, "some follow."

Tacha looked over at him, hunched over his sewing. "Why can Frank Shelby do whatever he wants?"

"Not everything, he can't."

"Why can he go in there with her?"

"Ask him when he's through."

"Do you know something?" Tacha said. "You never answer a question."

"I've been here—" the tailor began, and stopped as the outside door opened.

Bob Fisher stepped inside. He closed the door quietly behind him, his gaze going to the stock room, then to Tacha and past her to the tailor.

"Where's Norma at?"

Tacha waited. When she knew the tailor wasn't going to answer she said, "Don't you know where she is?"

Fisher's dull expression returned to Tacha. "I ask a question, I don't need a question back."

"She's in there," Tacha said.

"I thought I saw a convict come in here."

"He's in there with her."

"Doing what?"

"Doing *it*," Tacha said. "What do you think?"

Bob Fisher took time to give her a look before he walked over to the stock room. Then he didn't hesitate: he pushed the door and let it bang wide open and stood looking at them on the flat bolts of striped prison material they had spread on the floor, at the two of them lying close and pulling apart, at their upturned faces that were momentarily startled.

"You through?" Fisher said.

Shelby started to grin and shake his head. "I guess you caught us, boss."

Tacha could see Norma's skirt pulled up and her bare thighs. She saw Shelby, behind Fisher, getting to his feet. He was buttoning the top of his pants now. Norma was sitting up, slowly buttoning her blouse, then touching her hair, brushing it away from her face.

Tacha and the tailor began working again as Fisher looked around at them. He motioned Norma to get up. "You go on to your cell till I'm ready for you."

Shelby waited, while Norma gave Fisher a look and a shrug and walked out. He said then, "Were me and her doing something wrong? Against regulations?"

"You come with me," Fisher said.

Once outside, they moved off across the yard, toward the far end of the mess hall. Fisher held his set expression as his gaze moved about the yard. Shelby couldn't figure him out.

"Where we going?"

"I want to tell the new superintendent what you were doing."

"I didn't know of any law against it."

Fisher kept walking.

"What's going on?" Shelby said. Christ, the man was actually taking him in. Before they got to the latrine adobe Shelby said, "Well, I wanted to talk to him anyway." He paused. "About this guard that watches the girls take their bath. Pulls loose a brick and peeks in at them."

Fisher took six strides before saying, "She know who this guard is?"

"You bet," Shelby said.

"Then tell the sup'rintendent."

Son of a bitch. He was bluffing. Shelby glanced at him, but couldn't tell a thing from the man's expression.

Just past the latrine Shelby said, "I imagine this guard has got a real eyeful, oh man, but looking ain't near anything like doing, I'll tell you, 'cause I've done both. That Norma has got a natural-born instinct for pleasing a man. You know what she does?"

Fisher didn't answer.

Shelby waited, but not too long. "She knows secret things I bet there ain't ten women in the world can do. I been to Memphis, I been to Tulsa, to Nogales, I know what I'm talking about. You feel her mouth brushing your face and whispering dirty things in your ear—you know something? Once a man's had some of that woman—I mean somebody outside—he'd allow himself to be locked up in this place the rest of his life if he thought he could get some every other night. Get her right after she comes out of the bath."

Shelby paused to let Fisher think about it. As they were nearing the outside stairs he said, "Man, I tell you, anybody seen her bare-ass naked knows that's got to be a woman built for pleasure."

"Upstairs," Fisher said.

Shelby went up two steps and paused, looking around over his shoulder. "The thing is, though. She don't give it out to nobody but me. Less I say it's all right." Shelby looked right at his eyes. "You understand me, boss?"

Mr. Manly heard them coming down the hall. He swiveled around from the window and moved the two file folders to one side of the desk, covering the Bible. He picked up a pencil. On his note pad were written the names *Harold Jackson* and *Raymond San Carlos*, both underlined, and the notations: *Ten days will be Feb. 23, 1909. Talk to both at same time. Ref. to St. Paul to the Corinthians 11:19–33 and 12:1–9.*

When the knock came he said, "Come in" at once, but didn't look up until he knew they were in the room, close to the desk, and he had written on the note paper: *See Ephesians 4:1–6.*

Bob Fisher came right out with it. "He wants to tell you something."

In that moment Shelby had no idea what he would say; because Fisher wasn't bluffing and wasn't afraid of him; because Fisher stood up and was a tough son of a bitch and wasn't going to lie and lose face in front of any con. Maybe Fisher would deny the accusation, say prove it. Shelby didn't know what Fisher would do. He needed time to think. The next moment Mr. Manly was smiling up at him.

"I'm sorry I don't know everybody's name yet."

"This is Frank Shelby," Fisher said. "He wants to tell you something."

Shelby watched the little man rise and offer his hand and say, "I'm Everett Manly, your new superintendent." He watched Mr. Manly sit down again and look off somewhere.

"Frank Shelby . . . Shelby . . . forty-five years for armed robbery. Is that right?"

Shelby nodded.

"Forty-five years," Mr. Manly said. "That's a long time. Are you working to get some time off for good behavior?"

"I sure am," Shelby said. He didn't know if the man was serious or not, but he said it.

"How long have you been here at Yuma?"

"Little over a year."

"Have you got a good record here? Keep out of fights and trouble?"

"Yes, *sir*."

"Ever been in the snake den?"

"No, sir."

"Got two boys in there now for fighting, you know."

Shelby smiled a little and shook his head. "It's funny you should mention them," he said. "Those two boys are what I wanted to talk to you about."

Bob Fisher turned to look at him but didn't say a word.

"I was wondering," Shelby went on, "what you'd think of us staging a prize fight between those two boys?"

"A prize fight?" Mr. Manly frowned. "Don't you think they've done enough fighting? Lord, it seems all they like to do is fight."

"They keep fighting," Shelby said, "because they never get it settled. But, I figure, once they have it out there'll be peace between them. You see what I mean?"

Mr. Manly began to nod, slowly. "Maybe."

"We could get them some boxing gloves in town. I don't mean the prison pay for them. We could take us up a collection among the convicts."

"I sure never thought of fighting as a way to achieve peace. Bob, have you?"

Fisher said quietly, "No, I haven't."

Shelby shrugged. "Well, peace always seems to follow a war."

"You got a point there, Frank."

"I know the convicts would enjoy it. I mean it would keep their minds occupied a while. They don't get much entertainment here."

"That's another good point," Mr. Manly said.

Shelby waited as Mr. Manly nodded, looking as if he was falling asleep. "Well, that's all I had to say. I sure hope you give it some thought, if just for the sake of those two boys. So they can get it settled."

"I promise you I will," Mr. Manly said. "Bob, what do you think about it? Off-hand."

"I been in prison work a long time," Fisher said. "I never heard of anything like this."

"I'll tell you what, boys. Let me think on it." Mr. Manly got up out of the chair, extending a hand to Shelby. "It's nice meeting you, Frank. You keep up the good work and you'll be out of here before you know it."

"Sir," Shelby said, "I surely hope so."

Bob Fisher didn't say a word until they were down the stairs and Shelby was heading off along the side of the building, in the shade.

"Where you going?"

Shelby turned, a few steps away. "See about some chow."

"You can lose your privileges," Fisher said. "All of them inside one minute."

Go easy, Shelby thought, and said, "It's up to you."

"I can give it all to somebody else. The stuff you sell, the booze, the soft jobs. I pick somebody, the tough boys will side with him and once it's done he's the man inside and you're another con on the rock pile."

"I'm not arguing with you," Shelby said. "I used my head and put together what I got. You allow it because I keep the cons in line and it makes your job easier. You didn't give me a thing when I started."

"Maybe not, but I can sure take it all away from you."

"I know that."

"I will, less you stay clear of Norma Davis."

Shelby started to smile—he couldn't help it—even with Fisher's grim, serious face staring at him.

"Watch yourself," Fisher said. "You say the wrong thing, it's done. I'm telling you to keep away from the women. You don't, you lose everything you got."

That was all Bob Fisher had to say. He turned and went back up the stairs. Shelby watched him, feeling better than he'd felt in days. He sure would keep away from the women. He'd give Norma all the room she needed. The state Bob Fisher was in, Norma would have his pants off him before the week was out.

6

"Boys, I tell you the Lord loves us all as His children; but you cross Him and He can be mean as a roaring lion. Not mean because he hates you boys, no-sir; mean because he hates sin and evil so much. You don't believe me, read your Psalms, fifty, twenty-two, where it says, 'Now consider this, ye that forget God, lest I tear you in pieces'—you hear that?—'tear you in *pieces* and there be none to deliver. . . . ' None to deliver means there ain't nothing left of you."

Mr. Manly couldn't tell a thing from their expressions. Sometimes they were looking at him, sometimes they weren't. Their heads didn't move much. Their eyes did. Raymond's eyes would go to the window and stay there a while. Harold would stare at the wall or the bookcase, and look as if he was asleep with his eyes open.

Mr. Manly flipped back a few pages in his Bible. When he looked up again his glasses gleamed in the overhead light. He had brought the two boys out of the snake den after only three days this time. Bob Fisher hadn't said a word. He'd marched them over, got them fed and cleaned up, and here they were. Here, but somewhere else in their minds. Standing across the desk fifteen, twenty minutes now, and Mr. Manly wondered if either of them had listened to a word he'd said.

"Again in the Psalms, boys, chapter eleven, sixth verse, it says, 'Upon the wicked shall rain snares, fire and brimstone and a horrible tempest'—that's like a storm—'and this shall be the portion of their cup.'

"Raymond, look at me. 'He that keepeth the commandments keepeth his own soul'—Proverbs, chapter nineteen, verse sixteen—'but he that despiseth His way shall die.'

"Harold Jackson of Fort Valley, Georgia, 'There shall be no reward for the evil man.' That's Proverbs again, twenty-four, twenty. 'The candle of the wicked shall be put out.' Harold, you understand that?"

"Yes-suh, captain."

"What does it mean?"

"It mean they put out your candle."

"It means God will put *you* out. You're the candle, Harold. If you're evil you get no reward and the Lord God will snuff out your life. You want that to happen?"

"No-suh, captain."

"Raymond, you want to have your life snuffed out?"

"No, sir, I don't want no part of that."

"It will happen as sure as it is written in the Book. Harold, you believe in the Book?"

"What book is that, captain?"

"The Holy Bible."

"Yes-suh, I believe it."

"Raymond, you believe it?"

"What is that again?"

"Do you believe in the Holy Bible as being the in-spired word of Almighty God as told by Him directly into the ears of the boys that wrote it?"

"I guess so," Raymond said.

"Raymond, you don't guess about your salvation. You believe in Holy Scripture and its truths, or you don't."

"I believe it," Raymond said.

"Have you ever been to church?"

"I think so. When I was little."

"Harold, you ever attend services?"

"You mean was I in the arm service, captain?"

"I mean have you ever been to church."

"Yes, I been there, captain."

"When was the last time?"

"Let's see," Harold said. "I think I went in Cuba one time."

"You *think* you went to church?"

"They talk in this language I don't know what they saying, captain."

"That was ten years ago," Mr. Manly said, "and you don't know if it was a church service or not."

"I think it was."

"Raymond, what about you?"

"Yes, sir, when I was little, all the time."

"What do you remember?"

"About Jesus and all. You know, how they nail him to this cross."

"Do you know the Ten Commandments?"

"I think I know some of them," Raymond said. "Thou shall not steal. Thou shall not commit adultery."

"Thou shalt not kill," Mr. Manly prompted.

"Thou shall not kill. That's one of them."

"The one that sent you here. Both of you. And now you're disobeying that commandment again by fighting. Did you know that? When you fight you break the Lord's commandment against killing?"

"What if you only hit him?" Raymond asked. "Beat him up good, but he don't die."

"It's the same thing. Look, when you hit somebody you hurt him a little bit or you hurt him a lot. When you kill somebody you hurt him for good. So hitting is the same as killing without going all the way. You understand that, Harold?"

"What was that, captain?"

Mr. Manly swiveled around slowly to look out the window, toward the convicts standing by the main cellblock. Close to a hundred men here, and only a handful of them, at the most, understood the Divine Word. Mr. Manly was sixty years old and knew he would never have time to teach them all. He only had a few months here before the place was closed. Then what? He had to do what he could, that's all. He had to begin somewhere, even if his work was never finished.

He came around again to face them and said, "Boys, the Lord has put it on the line to us. He says you got to keep His commandments. He says you don't keep them, you die. That doesn't mean you die and they put in a grave—no-sir. It means you die and go straight down to

104

hell to suffer the fires of the damned. Raymond, you ever burn yourself?"

"Yes, sir, my hand one time."

"Boys, imagine getting burned all over for the rest of your life by the hottest fire you ever saw, hotter'n a blast furnace."

"You'd die," Raymond said.

"Only it doesn't kill you," Mr. Manly said quickly. "See, it's a special kind of fire that hurts terrible but never burns you up."

They looked at him, or seemed to be looking at him; he wasn't sure.

He tried again. "Like just your head is sticking out of the fire. You understand? So it don't suffocate you. But, boy, these flames are licking at your body and it's so hot you're a-screaming your lungs out, 'Water, water, somebody give me just a drop of water—please!' But it's too late, because far as you're concerned the Lord is fresh out of mercy."

Raymond was looking at the window again and Harold was studying the wall.

"Hell—" Mr. Manly began. He was silent for a while before he said, "It's a terrible place to be and I'm glad you boys are determined not to go there."

Harold said, "Where's that, captain?"

After they were gone Mr. Manly could still see them standing there. He got up and walked around them, picturing them from the back now, seeing the Negro's heavy, sloping shoulders, the Indian standing with a slight cock to his hip, hands loose at his sides. He'd like to stick a pin in them to see if they jumped. He'd like to holler in their ears. What's the matter with you? Don't you understand plain English? Are you too ignorant, or are you too full of evil? Answer me!

If they didn't understand the Holy Word, how was he ever going to preach it to them? He raised his eyes to the high ceiling and said, "Lord, if You're going to send me sinners, send me some with schooling, will you, please?"

He hadn't meant to say it out loud. In the silence that followed he hurried around the desk to sit down again.

Maybe that was the answer, though, and saying it out loud was the sign. Save somebody else, somebody who'd understand him, instead of two boys who couldn't even read and write. Sixty years old, he didn't have time to start saving illiterates. Somebody like Frank Shelby. Save him.

No, Frank was already trying. It was pretty clear he'd seen the error of his past life and was trying to correct it.

Norma Davis.

Get Norma in here and ask her if she was ready to accept the Lord Jesus Christ as her saviour. If she hadn't already.

No, something told Mr. Manly she hadn't yet. She was in for robbery, had shot a man, and had been arrested for prostitution in Wichita, Kansas. It wasn't likely she'd had time to be saved. She looked smart though.

Sit her down there, Mr. Manly thought.

He wasn't sure how he'd begin, but he'd get around

to picking some whores out of the Bible to tell her about—like that woman at the well. Jesus knew she was a whore, but He was still friendly and talked to her. See, He wasn't uppity about whores, they were just sinners to him like any other sinners. Take the time they're stoning the whore and He stops them, saying, Wait, only whoever of ye is without sin may cast a stone. And they had to quit doing it. See, Norma, we are all of us sinners in one way or another.

He kept looking at the way her top buttons were undone and the blouse was pulled open so he could see part of the valley between her breasts.

Where the soap had run down and over her belly.

She was sitting there trying to tempt him. Sure, she'd try to tempt him, try to show him up as a hypocrite.

She would undo a couple more buttons and he'd watch her calmly. He would say quietly, shaking his head slowly, "Norma, Norma."

She'd pull that blouse wide open and her eyes and her breasts would be staring right smack at him.

Sit back in the swivel chair then; show her he was at ease. Keep the expression very calm. And kindly.

She'd get up and lean over the desk then so they'd hang down. Great big round things with big reddish-brown tips. Then she'd jiggle them a little and he'd say in his quiet voice, "Norma, what are you doing that for? Don't you feel silly?"

Maybe he wouldn't ask her if she felt silly, but he'd say something.

She'd see she wasn't getting him, so then she'd take off her belt and slowly undo her skirt, watching him all the time, and let it fall. She'd back off a little bit and put her hands on her hips so he could see her good.

"Norma, child, cover your nakedness."

No, sir, that wasn't going to stop her. She was coming around the desk now. She'd stepped out of the skirt and was taking off the blouse, all the way off, coming toward him now without a stitch on.

He had better stand up, or it would be hard to talk to her.

Mr. Manly rose from the chair. He reached out to place his hands on Norma's bare shoulders and, smiling gently, said, "Child, 'If ye live after the flesh ye shall die'—Romans, eight, thirteen—'but if ye mortify the deeds of the body, ye shall live.' "

From the doorway Bob Fisher said, "Excuse me."

Mr. Manly came around, seeing the open door that had been left open when the two went out; he dropped his hands awkwardly to the edge of the desk.

Bob Fisher kept staring at him.

"I was just seeing if I could remember a particular verse from Romans," Mr. Manly said.

"How'd you do with Harold and Raymond?"

"It's too early to tell. I want to see them again in the morning."

"They got work to do."

"In the morning," Mr. Manly said.

Bob Fisher thought it over, then nodded and left the office. Walking down the hall, he was thinking that the little preacher may have been trying to remember a verse, but he sure looked like a man about to get laid.

* * *

Lord, give me these two, Mr. Manly said to the window and to the yard below. Give me a sign that they understand and are willing to receive the Lord Jesus Christ into their hearts.

He didn't mean a tongue of fire had to appear over the two boys' heads, or they had to get knocked to the ground the way St. Paul did. All they had to do was show some interest, a willingness to accept their salvation.

Lord, I need these two to prove my worthiness and devotion as a preacher of your Holy Writ. I need them to show for thirty years service in your ministry. Lord, I need them for my record, and I expect You know it.

Sit them down this time. Maybe that would help. Mr. Manly turned from the window and told them to take chairs. "Over there," he said. "Bring them up close to the desk."

They hesitated, looking around. It seemed to take them forever to carry the chairs over, their leg chains clinking on the wooden floor. He waited until they were settled, both of them looking past him, seeing what there was to see at this lower angle than yesterday.

"I'm going to tell you something. I know you both had humble beginnings. You were poor, you've been hungry, you've experienced all kinds of hardships and you've spent time in jail. Well, I never been to jail before I got sent here by the Bureau"—Mr. Manly paused as he grinned; neither of them noticing it—"I'll tell you though, I'll bet you I didn't begin any better off than you boys did. I was born in Clayburn County, Tennessee—either of you been there?"

Raymond shook his head. Harold said nothing.

"Well, it's in the mountains. I didn't visit Knoxville till I was fifteen years old, and it wasn't forty miles from home. I could've stayed there and farmed, or I could have run off and got into trouble. But you know what I did? I joined the Holy Word Pentacostal Youth Crusade and pledged myself to the service of the Lord Jesus. I preached over twenty years in Tennessee and Kentucky before coming out here to devote the rest of my life to mission work—the rest of it, five years, ten years. You know when your time is up and the Lord's going to call you?"

Harold Jackson's eyes were closed.

"Harold"—the eyes came open—"you don't know when you're going to die, do you?"

"No-suh, captain."

"Are you ready to die?"

"No-suh, captain. I don't think I ever be ready."

"St. Paul was ready."

"Yes-suh."

"Not at first he wasn't. Not until the Lord knocked him smack off his horse with a bolt of lightning and said, 'Saul, Saul, why do you persecuteth me?' Paul was a Jew-boy at that time and he was persecuting the Christians. Did you know that, Raymond?"

"No, I never knew that."

"Yes, sir, before he became Paul he was a Jew-boy name of Saul, used to put Christians to death, kill them in terrible ways. But once he become a Christian himself he made up for all the bad things he'd done by his own suffering. Raymond, you ever been stoned?"

"Like with rocks?"

"Hit with big rocks."

"I don't think so."

"Harold, you ever been shipwrecked?"

"I don't recall, captain."

Mr. Manly opened his Bible. "You boys think you've experienced hardships, listen, I'm going to read you something. From two Corinthians. 'Brethren, gladly you put up with fools, because you are wise . . . ' Let me skip down. 'But whereas any man is bold . . . Are they ministers of Christ?' Here it is ' . . . in many more labors, in lashes above measure, often exposed to death. From the Jews'—listen to this—'five times I received forty lashes less one. Thrice I was scourged, once I was stoned, thrice I suffered shipwreck, a night and a day I was adrift on the sea; on journeyings often, in perils from floods, in perils from robbers, in perils from my own nation . . . in labor and hardships, in many sleepless nights, in hunger and thirst, in fastings often, in cold and nakedness.' "

Mr. Manly looked up. "Here's the thing, boys. St. Paul asked God three times to let him up from all these hardships. And you know what God said to him?" Mr. Manly's gaze dropped to the book. "He said, 'My grace is sufficient for thee, for strength is made perfect in weakness.' "

Now Mr. Manly sat back, just barely smiling, looking expectantly from Raymond to Harold, waiting for one of them to speak. Either one, he didn't care.

He didn't even care what they said, as long as one of them spoke.

Raymond was looking down at his hands, fooling with one of his fingernails. Harold was looking down too, his head bent low, and his eyes could have been open or closed.

"Strength—did you hear that, boys?—is made perfect in weakness."

He waited.

He could ask them what it meant.

He began thinking about the words. If you're weak the Lord helps you. Or strength stands out more in a weak person. Like it's more perfect, more complete, when a weak person gets strong.

No, that wasn't what it meant.

It meant no matter how weak you were you could get strong if you wanted.

Maybe. Or else it was the part just before which was the important part. God saying My grace is sufficient for thee. That's right, no matter what the temptaion was.

Norma Davis could come in here and show herself and do all kinds of terrible things—God's grace would be sufficient. That was good to know.

It wasn't helping those two boys any, though. He had to watch that, thinking of himself more than them. They were the ones had to be saved. They had wandered from the truth and it was up to him to bring them back. For . . . 'whoever brings back a sinner from the error of his ways will save his own soul from death'—James, five-something—'and it will cover a multitude of sins.' "

That was the whole thing. If he could save these two boys he'd have nothing to worry about the rest of his life. He could maybe even slip once in a while—give in to temptation—without fear of his soul getting sent to hell. He wouldn't give in on purpose. You couldn't do that. But if somebody dragged you in and you went in scrapping, that was different.

"Boys," Mr. Manly said, "whoever brings back a sinner saves his own soul from death and it will cover a multitude of sins. Now do you want your souls to be saved, or don't you?"

Mr. Manly spent two days reading and studying before he called Raymond and Harold into the office again.

While they were standing by the desk he asked them how they were getting along. Neither of them wanted to answer that. He asked if there had been any trouble between them since the last time they were here. They both said no, sir. He asked if there had been any mean words between them. They said no, sir. Then it looked like they were getting somewhere, Mr. Manly said, and told them to bring the chairs over and sit down.

" 'We know,' " he said to Raymond, " 'that we have passed from death unto life because we love the brethren. He that loveth not his brethren abideth in death.' " Mr. Manly looked at Harold Jackson. " 'Whoever hateth his brother is a murderer, and ye know that no murderer hath eternal life abiding in him.' James, chapter three, the fourteenth and fifteenth verses."

They were looking at him. That was good. They weren't squinting or frowning, as if they were trying to figure out the words, or nodding agreement; but by golly they were looking at him and not out the window.

"Brethren means brother," he said. "You know that.

113

It doesn't mean just your real brother, if you happen to have any brothers. It means everybody's your brethren. You two are brethren and I'm your brethren, everybody here at Yuma and everybody in the whole world, we are all brethren of Jesus Christ and sons of Almighty God. Even women. What I'm talking about, even women are your brethren, but we don't have to get into that. I'm saying we are all related by blood and I'll tell you why. You listening?"

Raymond's gaze came away from the window, his eyes opening wide with interest.

Harold said, "Yes-suh, captain."

"We are all related," Mr. Manly said, watching them, "because we all come from the first two people in the world, old Adam and Eve, who started the human race. They had children and their children had children and the children's children had some more, and it kept going that way until the whole world become populated."

Harold Jackson said, "Who did the children marry?"

"They married each other."

"I mean children in the same family."

Mr. Manly nodded. "Each other. They married among theirselves."

"You mean a boy did it with his sister?"

"Oh," Mr. Manly said. "Yes, but it was different then. God said it was all right because it was the only way to get the earth populated. See, in just a few generations you got so many people they're marrying cousins now, and second cousins, and a couple hundred years it's not even like they're kin any more."

Mr. Manly decided not to tell them about Adam living to be nine hundred and thirty and Seth and Enoch and Kenan and Methuselah, all of them getting up past nine hundred years old before they died. He had to leave out details or it might confuse them. It was enough to tell them how the population multiplied and the people gradually spread all over the world.

"If we all come from the same people," Raymond said, "where do niggers come from?"

So Mr. Manly had to tell them about Noah and his three sons, Shem, Ham, and Japheth, and how Ham made some dirty remark on seeing his daddy sleeping naked after drinking too much wine. For that Noah banished Ham and made his son a "slave of slaves." Ham and his family had most likely gone on down to Africa and that was where niggers came from, descendents of Ham.

Harold Jackson said, "Where does it say Indins come from?"

Mr. Manly shook his head. "It don't say and it don't matter. People moved all over the world, and those living in a certain place got to look alike on account of the climate. So now you got your white race, your yellow race, and your black race."

"What's an Indin?" Harold said. "What race?"

"They're not sure," Mr. Manly answered. "Probably somewhere in between. Like yellow with a little nigger thrown in. You can call it the Indian race if you want. The colored race is the only one mentioned in the Bible, on account of the story of Noah and Ham."

Harold said, "How do they know everybody was white before that?"

Mr. Manly frowned. What kind of a question was that? "They just know it. I guess because Adam and Eve was white." He said then, "There's nothing wrong with being a nigger. God made you a nigger for a reason. I mean some people have to be niggers and some have to be Indians. Some have to be white. But we are all still brethren."

Harold's eyes remained on Mr. Manly. "It say in the Bible this man went to Africa?"

"It wasn't called Africa then, but they're pretty sure that's where he went. His people multiplied and before you know it they're living all over Africa and that's how you got your different tribes. Your Zulus. Your Pygmies. You got your—oh, all different ones with those African names."

"Zulus," Harold Jackson said. "I heard something about Zulus one time."

Mr. Manly leaned forward on the edge of the desk. "What did you hear about them?"

"I don't know. I remember somebody talking about Zulus. Somebody saying the word."

"Harold, you know something? For all you know you might be a Zulu yourself."

Harold gave him a funny look. "I was born in Fort Valley, Georgia."

"Where was your mama and daddy born?"

"Fort Valley."

"Where was your granddaddy born?"

"I don't know."

"Or your great-granddaddy. You know, he might have been born in Africa and brought over here as a slave. Maybe not him, but somebody before him, a kin of yours, was brought over. All your kin before him lived in Africa, and if they lived in a certain part of Africa then, by golly, they were Zulus."

Mr. Manly had a book about Africa in his collection. He remembered a drawing of a Zulu warrior, a tall Negro standing with a spear and a slender black and white cowhide shield.

He said, "Harold, your people are fine hunters and warriors. Oh, they're heathen, they paint theirselves up red and yellow and wear beads made out of lion's claws; but, Harold, they got to kill the lion first, with spears, and you don't go out and kill a lion unless you got plenty of nerve."

"With a spear, huh?" Harold said.

"Long spear they use, and this shield made out of cowhide. Some of them grow little beards and cut holes in the lobes of their ears and stick in these big hunks of dried sugar cane, if I remember correctly."

"They have sugar cane?"

"That's what it said in the book."

"They had a lot of sugar cane in Cuba. I never see anybody put it in their ear."

"Like earrings," Mr. Manly said. "I imagine they use all kinds of things. Gold, silver, if they got it."

"What do they wear?"

"Oh, just a little skimpy outfit. Some kind of cloth or animal skin around their middle. Nothing up here. Wait a second," Mr. Manly said. He went over to his bookcase. He found the book right away, but had to skim through it twice before he found the picture and laid the book open in front of Harold. "There. That's your Zulu warrior."

Harold hunched over the book. As he studied the picture Mr. Manly said, "Something else I remember. It says in there these Zulus can run. I mean *run*. The boys training to be warriors, they'd run twenty miles, take a little rest and run some more. Run thirty-forty miles a day isn't anything for a Zulu. Then go out and kill a lion. Or a elephant."

Mr. Manly noticed Raymond San Carlos glancing over at the book and he said quickly, "Same with your Indians; especially your desert tribes, like the Apaches. They can run all day long, I understand, and not take a drink of water till sundown. They know where to find water, too, way out in the middle of the desert. Man told me once, when Apaches are going where they know there isn't any water they take a horse's intestine and fill it full of water and wrap it around their bodies. He said he'd match an Apache Indian against a camel for traveling across the desert without any water."

"There's plenty of water," Raymond said, "if you know where to look."

"That's what I understand."

"Some of the older men at San Carlos, they'd take us boys and make us go up in the mountains and stay there two, three days without food or water."

"You did that?"

"Plenty of times."

"You'd find water?"

"Sure, and something to eat. Not much, but enough to hold us."

"Say, I just read in the paper," Mr. Manly said. "You know who died the other day? Geronimo."

"Is that right?"

"Fort Sill, Oklahoma. Died of pneumonia."

"That's too bad," Raymond said. "I mean I think he would rather have got killed fighting."

"You ever seen him? No, you would have been too young."

"Sure, I seen him. Listen, I'll tell you something I never told anybody. My father was in his band. Geronimo's."

"Is that a fact?"

"He was killed in Mexico when the soldiers went down there."

"My goodness," Mr. Manly said, "we're talking about warriors, you're the son of an Apache warrior."

"I never told anybody that."

"Why not? I'd think you'd be proud to tell it."

"It doesn't do me any good."

"But if it's true—"

"You think I'm lying?"

"I mean since it's a fact, why not tell it?"

"It don't make any difference to me. I could be Apache, I could be Mexican, I'm in Yuma the rest of my life."

"But you're living that life," Mr. Manly said. "If a person's an Indian then he should look at himself as an Indian. Like I told Harold, God made him a nigger for a reason. All right, God made you an Indian. There's nothing wrong with being an Indian. Why, do you know that about half our states have Indian names? Mississippi.

The state I come from, Tennessee. Arizona. The Colorado River out yonder. Yuma."

"I don't know," Harold said, "that spear looks like it could break easy."

Mr. Manly looked over at him and at the book. "They know how to make 'em."

"They fight other people?"

"Sure they did. Beat 'em, too. What I understand, your Zulus owned most of the southern part of Africa, took it from other tribes and ruled over them."

"Never got beat, uh?"

"Not that I ever heard of. No, sir, they're the greatest warriors in Africa."

"Nobody ever beat the Apache," Raymond said, "till the U. S. Army come with all their goddamn guns."

"Raymond, don't ever take the Lord's name in vain like that."

"Apaches beat the Pimas, the Papagos, Maricopas—took anything we wanted from them."

"Well, I don't hold with raiding and killing," Mr. Manly said, "but I'll tell you there is something noble about your uneducated savage that you don't see in a lot of white men. I mean just the way your warrior stands, up straight with his shoulders back and never says too much, doesn't talk just to hear himself, like a lot of white people I know. I'll tell you something else, boys. Savage warriors have never been known to lie or go back on their word, and that's a fact. Man up at the reservation told me that Indians don't even have a word in their language for lie. Same thing with your Zulus. I reckon if a boy can run all day long and kill lions with a spear, he don't ever *have* to lie."

"I never heard of Apaches with spears," Raymond said.

"Oh, yes, they had them. And bows and arrows."

Harold was waiting. "I expect the Zulus got guns now, don't they?"

"I don't know about that," Mr. Manly answered. "Maybe they don't need guns. Figure spears are good enough." A smile touched his mouth as he looked across the desk at Raymond and Harold. "The thing that tickles me," he said, "I'm liable to have a couple of real honest-to-goodness Apache and Zulu warriors sitting right here in my office and I didn't even know it."

That evening, when Bob Fisher got back after supper, the guard at the sally port told him Mr. Manly wanted to see him right away. Fisher asked him what for, and the guard said how was he supposed to know. Fisher told the man to watch his mouth, and headed across the compound to see what the little squirt wanted.

Fisher paused by the stairs and looked over toward the cook shack. The women would be starting their bath about now.

Mr. Manly was writing something, but put it aside as Fisher came in. He said, "Pull up a chair," and seemed anxious to talk.

"There's a couple of things I got to do yet tonight."

"I wanted to talk to you about our Apache and our Zulu."

"How's that?"

"Raymond and Harold. I've been thinking about Frank Shelby's idea—he seems like a pretty sensible young man, doesn't he?"

Jesus Christ, Bob Fisher thought. He said, "I guess he's smart enough."

Mr. Manly smiled. "Though not smart enough to stay out of jail. Well, I've been thinking about this boxing-match idea. I want you to know I've given it a lot of thought."

Fisher waited.

"I want Frank Shelby to understand it too—you might mention it to him if you see him before I do."

"I'll tell him," Fisher said. He started to go.

"Hey, I haven't told you what I decided."

Fisher turned to the desk again.

"I've been thinking—a boxing match wouldn't be too good. We want them to stop fighting and we tell them to go ahead and fight. That doesn't sound right, does it?"

"I'll tell him that."

"You're sure in a hurry this evening, Bob."

"It's time I made the rounds is all."

"Well, I could walk around with you if you want and we could talk."

"That's all right," Fisher said, "go ahead."

"Well, as I said, we won't have the boxing match. You know what we're going to have instead?"

"What?"

"We're going to have a race. I mean Harold and Raymond are going to have a race."

"A race," Fisher said.

"A foot race. The faster man wins and gets some kind of a prize, but I haven't figured that part of it out yet."

"They're going to run a race," Fisher said.

"Out in the exercise yard. Down to the far end and back, maybe a couple of times."

"When do you want this race held?"

"Tomorrow I guess, during free time."

"You figure it'll stop them fighting, uh?"

"We don't have anything to lose," Mr. Manly said. "A good race might just do the trick."

Get out of here, Bob Fisher thought. He said, "Well, I'll tell them."

"I've already done that."

"I'll tell Frank Shelby then." Fisher edged toward the door and got his hand on the knob.

"You know what it is?" Mr. Manly was leaning back in his chair with a peaceful, thoughtful expression. "It's sort of a race of races," he said. "You know what I mean? The Negro against the Indian, black man against red man. I don't mean to prove that one's better than the other. I mean as a way to stir up their pride and get them interested in doing something with theirselves. You know what I mean?"

Bob Fisher stared at him.

"See, the way I figure them—" Mr. Manly motioned to the chair again. "Sit down, Bob, I'll tell you how I see these two boys, and why I believe we can help them."

By the time Fisher got down to the yard, the women had taken their bath. They were back in their cellblock and he had to find R. E. Baylis for the keys.

"I already locked everybody in," the guard said.

"I know you did. That's why I need the keys."

"Is there something wrong somewhere?"

Bob Fisher had never wanted to look at that woman as bad as he did this evening. God, he felt like he *had* to look at her, but everybody was getting in his way, wasting time. His wife at supper nagging at him again about moving to Florence. The little squirt preacher who believed he could save a couple of bad convicts. Now a slow-witted guard asking him questions.

"Just give me the keys," Fisher said.

He didn't go over there directly. He walked past the TB cellblock first and looked in at the empty yard, at the lantern light showing in most of the cells and the dark ovals of the cells that were not occupied. The nigger and the Indian were in separate cells. They were doing a fair job on the wall; but, Jesus, they'd get it done a lot sooner if the little squirt would let them work instead of wasting time preaching to them. Now foot races. God Almighty.

Once you were through the gate of the women's cellblock, the area was more like a room than a yard—a little closed-in courtyard and two cells carved into the granite wall.

There was lantern light in both cells. Fisher looked in at Tacha first and asked her what she was doing. Tacha was sitting on a stool in the smoky dimness of the cell. She said, "I'm reading," and looked down at the book again. Bob Fisher told himself to take it easy now and not to be impatient. He looked in Tacha's cell almost a minute longer before moving on to Norma's.

She was stretched out in her bunk, staring right at

him when he looked through the iron strips of the door. A blanket covered her, but one bare arm and shoulder were out of the blanket and, Jesus, it didn't look like she had any clothes on. His gaze moved around the cell to show he wasn't too interested in her.

"Everything all right?"

"That's a funny thing to ask," Norma said. "Like this is a hotel."

"I haven't looked in here in a while."

"I know you haven't."

"You need another blanket or anything?"

"What's anything?"

"I mean like kerosene for the lantern."

"I think there's enough. The light's awful low though."

"Turn it up."

"I can't. I think the wick's stuck. Or else it's burned down."

"You want me to take a look at it?"

"Would you? I'd appreciate it."

Bob Fisher brought the ring of keys out of his coat pocket with the key to Norma's cell in his hand. As he opened the door and came in, Norma raised up on one elbow, holding the blanket in front of her. He didn't look at her; he went right to the lamp and peered in through the smoky glass. As he turned the wick up slowly, the light grew brighter, then dimmed again as he turned it down.

"It seems all right now." Fisher glanced at her, twisted bare back. He tried the lantern a few more times, twisting the wick up and down and knowing her bare back—and that meant her bare front too—wasn't four feet away from him. "It must've been stuck," he said.

"I guess it was. Will you turn it down now? Just so there's a nice glow."

"How's that?"

"That's perfect."

"I think you got enough wick in there."

"I think so. Do you want to get in bed with me?"

"Jesus Christ," Bob Fisher said.

"Well, do you?"

"You're a nervy thing, aren't you?"

Norma twisted around a little more and let the blanket fall. "I can't help it."

"You can't help what?"

"If I want you to do it to me."

"Jesus," Bob Fisher said. He looked at the cell door and then at Norma again, cleared his throat and said in a lower tone, "I never heard a girl asking for it before."

"Well," Norma said, throwing the blanket aside as she got up from the bunk and moved toward him, "you're hearing it now, daddy."

"Listen, Tacha's right next door."

"She can't see us."

"She can hear."

"Then we'll whisper." Norma began unbuttoning his coat.

"We can't do nothing here."

"Why not?"

"One of the guards might come by."

"Now you're teasing me. Nobody's allowed in here at night, and you know it."

"Boy, you got big ones."

"There, now slip your coat off."

"I can't stay here more'n a few minutes."

"Then quit talking," Norma said.

7

Frank Shelby said, "A race, what do you mean, a race?"

"I mean a foot race," Fisher told him. "The nigger and the Indin are going to run a race from one end of the yard to the other and back again, and you and every convict in this place are going to be out here to watch it."

"A race," Shelby said again. "Nobody cares about any foot race."

"You don't have to care," Fisher said. "I'm not asking you to care. I'm telling you to close your store and get everybody's ass out of the cellblock. They can stand here or over along the south wall. Ten minutes, I want everybody out."

"This is supposed to be our free time."

"I'll tell you when you get free time."

"What if we want to make some bets?"

"I don't care, long as you keep it quiet. I don't want any arguments, or have to hit anybody over the head."

"Ten minutes, it doesn't give us much time to figure out how to bet."

"You don't know who's going to win," Fisher said. "What's the difference?"

About half the convicts were already in the yard. Fisher waited for the rest of them to file out: the card players and the convicts who could afford Frank Shelby's whiskey and the ones who were always in their bunks between working and eating. They came out of the cellblock and stood around waiting for something to happen. The guards up on the wall came out of the towers and looked around too, as if they didn't know what was going on. Bob Fisher hadn't told any of them about the race. It wouldn't take more than a couple of minutes. He told the convicts to keep the middle area of the yard clear. They started asking him what was going on, but he walked away from them toward the mess hall. It was good that he did. When Mr. Manly appeared on the stairway at the end of the building Fisher was able to get to him before he reached the yard.

"You better stay up on the stairs."

Mr. Manly looked surprised. "I was going over there with the convicts."

"It's happened a sup'rintendent's been grabbed and a knife put at his throat till the gate was opened."

"You go among the convicts; all the guards do."

"But if any of us are grabbed the gate stays closed. They know that. They don't know about you."

"I just wanted to mingle a little," Mr. Manly said. He looked out toward the yard. "Are they ready?"

"Soon as they get their leg-irons off."

A few minutes later, Raymond and Harold were brought down the length of the yard. The convicts watched them, and a few called out to them. Mr. Manly didn't hear what they said, but he noticed neither Raymond nor Harold looked over that way. When they reached the stairs he said. "Well, boys, are you ready?"

"You want us to run," Raymond said. "You wasn't kidding, uh?"

"Course I wasn't."

"I don't know. We just got the irons off. My legs feel funny."

"You want to warm up first?"

Harold Jackson said, "I'm ready any time he is."

Raymond shrugged. "Let's run the race."

Mr. Manly made sure they understood—down to the end of the yard, touch the wall between the snake den and the women's cellblock, and come back past the stairs, a distance Mr. Manly figured to be about a hundred and twenty yards or so. He and Mr. Fisher would be at the top of the stairs in the judge's stand. Mr. Fisher would fire off a revolver as the starting signal. "So," Mr. Manly said, "if you boys are ready—"

There was some noise from the convicts as Raymond and Harold took off as the shot was fired and passed the main cellblock in a dead heat. Raymond hit the far wall and came off in one motion. Harold stumbled and dug hard on the way back but was five or six yards behind Raymond going across the finish.

They stood with their hands on their hips breathing in and out while Mr. Manly leaned over the rail of the stair landing, smiling down at them. He said, "Hey, boys, you sure gave it the old try. Rest a few minutes and we'll run it again."

Raymond looked over at Harold. They got down again and went off with the sound of the revolver, Raymond letting Harold set the pace this time, staying with him and not kicking out ahead until they were almost to the finish line. This time he took it by two strides, with the convicts yelling at them to *run*.

Raymond could feel his chest burning now. He walked around breathing with his mouth open, looking up at the sky that was fading to gray with the sun below the west wall, walking around in little circles and seeing Mr. Manly up there now. As Raymond turned away he heard Harold say, "Let's do it again," and he had to go along.

Harold dug all the way this time; he felt his thighs knotting and pushed it some more, down and back and, with the convicts yelling, came in a good seven strides ahead of the Indian. Right away Harold said, "Let's do it again."

In the fourth race he was again six or seven strides faster than Raymond.

In the fifth race, neither of them looked as if he was going to make it back to the finish. They ran pumping their arms and gasping for air, and Harold might have been ahead by a half-stride past the stairs; but Raymond stumbled and fell forward trying to catch himself, and it was hard to tell who won. There wasn't a sound from the convicts this time. Some of them weren't even looking this way. They were milling around, smoking cigarettes, talking among themselves.

Mr. Manly wasn't watching the convicts. He was leaning over the railing looking down at his two boys: at Raymond lying stretched out on his back and at Harold sitting, leaning back on his hands with his face raised to the sky.

"Hey, boys," Mr. Manly called, "you know what I want you to do now? First I want you to get up. Come on, boys, get up on your feet. Raymond, you hear me?"

"He looks like he's out," Fisher said.

"No, he's all right. See?"

Mr. Manly leaned closer over the rail. "Now I want you two to walk up to each other. Go on, do as I say. It won't hurt you. Now I want you both to reach out and shake hands. . . .

"Don't look up here. Look at each other and shake hands."

Mr. Manly started to grin and, by golly, he really felt good. "Bob, look at that."

"I see it," Fisher said.

Mr. Manly called out now, "Boys, by the time you get done running together you're going to be good friends. You wait and see."

The next day, while they were working on the face wall in the TB cellblock, Raymond was squatting down mixing mortar in a bucket and groaned as he got to his feet. "Goddamn legs," he said.

"I know what you mean," Harold said. He was laying a brick, tapping it into place with the handle of his trowel, and hesitated as he heard his own voice and realized he had spoken to Raymond. He didn't look over at him; he picked up another brick and laid it in place. It was quiet in the yard. The tubercular convicts were in their cells, out of the heat and the sun. Harold could hear a switch-engine working, way down the hill in the Southern Pacific yard; he could hear the freight cars banging together as they were coupled.

After a minute or so Raymond said, "I can't hardly walk today."

"From running," Harold said.

"They don't put the leg-irons back on, uh?"

"I wondered if they forgot to."

"I think so. They wouldn't leave them off unless they forgot."

There was silence again until Harold said, "They can leave them off, it's all right with me."

"Sure," Raymond said, "I don't care they leave them off."

"Place in Florida, this prison farm, you got to wear them all the time."

"Yeah? I hope I never get sent there."

"You ever been to Cuba?"

"No, I never have."

"That's a fine place. I believe I like to go back there sometime."

"Live there?"

"Maybe. I don't know."

"Look like we need some more bricks," Raymond said.

The convicts mixing the adobe mud straightened up with their shovels in front of them as Raymond and Harold came across the yard pushing their wheelbarrows. Joe Dean stepped around to the other side of the mud so he could keep an eye on the south-wall tower guard. He waited until the two boys were close, heading for the brick pile.

"Well, now," Joe Dean said, "I believe it's the two sweethearts."

"If they come back for some more," another convict said, "I'm going to cut somebody this time."

Joe Dean watched them begin loading the wheelbarrows. "See, what they do," he said. "they start a ruckus so they'll get sent to the snake den. Sure, they get in there, just the two of them. Man, they hug and kiss, do all kinds of things to each other."

"That is Mr. Joe Dean talking," Harold said. "I believe he wants to get hit in the mouth with a 'dobe brick."

"I want to see you try that," Joe Dean said.

"Sometime when the guard ain't looking," Harold said. "Maybe when you ain't looking either."

They finished loading their wheelbarrows and left.

In the mess hall at supper they sat across one end of a table. No one else sat with them. Raymond looked around at the convicts hunched over eating. No one seemed aware of them. They were all talking or concentrating on their food. He said to Harold, "Goddamn beans, they always got to burn them."

"I've had worse beans," Harold said. "Worse everything. What I like is some chicken, that's what I miss. Chicken's good."

"I like a beefsteak. With peppers and catsup."

"Beefsteak's good too. You like fried fish?"

"I never had it."

"You never had fish?"

"I don't think so."

"Man, where you been you never had fish?"

"I don't know, I never had it."

"We got a big river right outside."

"I never seen anybody fishing."

"How long it take you to swim across?"

"Maybe five minutes."

"That's a long time to swim."

"Too long. They get a boat out quick."

"Anybody try to dig out of here?"

"I never heard of it," Raymond said. "The ones that go they always run from a work detail, outside."

"Anybody make it?"

"Not since I been here."

"Man start running he got to know where he's going. He got to have a place to go to." Harold looked up from his plate. "How long you here for?"

"Life."

"That's a long time, ain't it?"

They were back at work on the cell wall the next day when a guard came and got them. It was about mid-afternoon. Neither of them asked where they were going; they figured they were going to hear another sermon from the man. They marched in front of the guard down the length of the yard and past the brick detail. When they got near the mess hall they veered a little toward the stairway and the guard said, "Keep going, straight ahead."

Raymond and Harold couldn't believe it. The guard marched them through the gates of the sally port and right up to Mr. Rynning's twenty-horsepower Ford Touring Car.

"Let me try to explain it to you again," Mr. Manly said to Bob Fisher. "I believe these boys have got to develop some pride in theirselves. I don't mean they're supposed to get uppity with us. I mean they got to look at theirselves as man in the sight of men, and children in the eyes of God."

"Well, I don't know anything about that part," Bob Fisher said. "To me they are a couple of bad cons, and if you want my advice based on years of dealing with these people, we put their leg-irons back on."

"They can't run in leg-irons."

"I know they can't. They need to work and they need to get knocked down a few times. A convict stands up to you, you better knock him down quick."

"Have they stood up to you, Bob?"

"One of them served time in Leavenworth, the other one tried to swim the river and they're both trying to kill one another. I call that standing up to me."

"You say they're hard cases, Bob, and I say they're like little children, because they're just now beginning to learn about living with their fellowman, which to them means living with white men and getting along with white men."

"Long as they're here," Fisher said, "they damn well better. We only got one set of rules."

Mr. Manly shook his head. "I don't mean to change the rules for them." It was harder to explain than he thought it would be. He couldn't look right at Fisher; the

man's solemn expression, across the desk, distracted
him. He would glance at Fisher and then look down at
the sheet of paper that was partly covered with oval
shapes that were like shields, and long thin lines that
curved awkwardly into spearheads. "I don't mean to
treat them as privileged characters either. But we're not
going to turn them into white men, are we?"

"We sure aren't."

"We're not going to tell them they're just as good as
white men, are we?"

"I don't see how we could do that," Fisher said.

"So we tell them what an Indian is good at and what
a nigger is good at."

"Niggers lie and Indians steal."

"Bob, we tell them what they're good at as members
of their race. We already got it started. We tell them Indians and niggers are the best runners in the world."

"I guess if they're scared enough."

"We train them hard and, by golly, they begin to believe it."

"Yeah?"

"Once they begin to believe in something, they begin
to believe in themselves."

"Yeah?"

"That's all there is to it."

"Well, maybe you ought to get some white boys to
run against them."

"Bob, I'm not interested in them running *races*. This
has got to do with distance and endurance. Being able to
do something no one else in this prison can do. That race
out in the yard was all wrong, more I think about it."

"Frank Shelby said he figured the men wouldn't mind seeing different kinds of races instead of just back and forth. He said run them all over and have them jump things—like climb up the wall on ropes, see who can get to the top first. He said he thought the men would get a kick out of that."

"Bob, this is a show. It doesn't prove nothing. I'm talking about these boys running *miles*."

"Miles, uh?"

"Like their granddaddies used to do."

"How's that?"

"Like Harold Jackson's people back in Africa. Bob, they kill lions with *spears*."

"Harold killed a man with a lead pipe."

"There," Mr. Manly said. "That's the difference. That's what he's become because he's forgot what it's like to be a Zulu nigger warrior."

Jesus Christ, Bob Fisher said to himself. The little squirt shouldn't be sitting behind the desk, he should be over in the goddamn crazy hole. He said, "You want them to run miles, uh?"

"Start them out a few miles a day. Work up to ten miles, twenty miles. We'll see how they do."

"Well, it will be something to see, all right, them running back and forth across the yard. I imagine the convicts will make a few remarks to them. The two boys get riled up and lose their temper, they're back in the snake den and I don't see you've made any progress at all."

"I've already thought of that," Mr. Manly said. "They're not going to run in the yard. They're going to run outside."

* * *

The convicts putting up the adobe wall out at the cemetery were the first ones to see them. A man raised up to stretch the kinks out of his back and said, "Look-it up there!"

They heard the Ford Touring Car as they looked around and saw it up on the slope, moving along the north wall with the two boys running behind it. Nobody could figure it out. Somebody asked what were they chasing the car for. Another convict said they weren't chasing the car, they were being taken somewhere. See, there was a guard in the back seat with a rifle. They could see him good against the pale wall of the prison. Nobody had ever seen convicts taken somewhere like that. Any time the car went out it went down to Yuma, but no convicts were ever in the car or behind it or anywhere near it. One of the convicts asked the work-detail guard where he supposed they were going. The guard said it beat him. That motor car belonged to Mr. Rynning and was only used for official business.

It was the stone-quarry gang that saw them next. They looked squinting up through the white dust and saw the Ford Touring Car and the two boys running to keep up with it, about twenty feet behind the car and just barely visible in all the dust the car was raising. The stone-quarry gang watched until the car was past the open rim and the only thing left to see was the dust hanging in the sunlight. Somebody said they certainly had it ass-backwards; the car was supposed to be chasing the cons. They tried to figure it out, but nobody had an answer that made much sense.

Two guards and two convicts, including Joe Dean, coming back in the wagon from delivering a load of adobe bricks in town, saw them next—saw them pass right by on the road—and Joe Dean and the other convict and the two guards turned around and watched them until the car crossed the railroad tracks and passed behind some depot sheds. Joe Dean said he could understand why the guards didn't want the spook and the Indian riding with them, but he still had never seen anything like it in all the time he'd been here. The guards said they had never seen anything like it either. There was funny things going on. Those two had raced each other, maybe they were racing the car now. Joe Dean said Goddamn, this was the craziest prison he had ever been in.

That first day, the best they could run in one stretch was a little over a mile. They did that once: down prison hill and along the railroad tracks and out back of town, out into the country. Most of the time, in the three hours they were out, they would run as far as they could, seldom more than a quarter of a mile—then have to quit and walk for a while, breathing hard with their mouths open and their lungs on fire. They would drop thirty to forty feet back of the car and the guard with the Winchester would yell at them to come on, get the lead out of their feet.

Harold said to Raymond, "I had any lead in my feet I'd take and hit that man in the mouth with it."

"We tell him we got to rest," Raymond said.

They did that twice, sat down at the side of the road

in the meadow grass and watched the guard coming with the rifle and the car backing up through its own dust. The first time the guard pointed the rifle and yelled for them to get on their feet. Harold told him they couldn't move and asked him if he was going to shoot them for being tired.

"Captain, we *want* to run, but our legs won't mind what we tell them."

So the guard gave them five minutes and they sat back in the grass to let their muscles relax and stared at the distant mountains while the guards sat in the car smoking their cigarettes.

Harold said to Raymond, "What are we doing this for?"

Raymond gave him a funny look. "Because we're tired, what do you think?"

"I mean running. What are we running for?"

"They say to run, we run."

"It's that little preacher."

"Sure it is. What do you think, these guards thought of it?"

"That little man's crazy, ain't he?"

"I don't know," Raymond said. "Most of the time I don't understand him. He's got something in his head about running."

"Running's all right if you in a hurry and you know where you going."

"That road don't go anywhere."

"What's up ahead?"

"The desert," Raymond said. "Maybe after a while you come to a town."

"You know how to drive that thing?"

"A car? I never even been in one."

Harold was chewing on a weed stem, looking at the car. "It would be nice to have a ride home, wouldn't it?"

"It might be worth the running," Raymond said.

The guard got them up and they ran some more. They ran and walked and ran again for almost another mile, and this time when they went down they stretched out full length: Harold on his stomach, head down and his arms propping him up; Raymond on his back with his chest rising and falling.

After ten minutes the guard said all right, they were starting back now. Neither of them moved as the car turned around and rolled past them. The guard asked if they heard him. He said goddamn-it, they better get up quick. Harold said captain, their legs hurt so bad it didn't look like they could make it. The guard levered a cartridge into the chamber of the Winchester and said their legs would hurt one hell of a lot more with a .44 slug shot through them. They got up and fell in behind the car. Once they tried to run and had to stop within a dozen yards. It wasn't any use, Harold said. The legs wouldn't do what they was told. They could walk though. All right, the guard said, then walk. But god-*damn*, they were so slow, poking along, he had to keep yelling at them to come on. After a while, still not in sight of the railroad tracks, the guard driving said to the other guard, if they didn't hurry they were going to miss supper call. The guard with the Winchester said well, what was he supposed to do about it? The guard driving said it looked like there was only one thing they *could* do.

Raymond liked it when the car stopped and the guard with the rifle, looking like he wanted to kill them, said all right, goddamn-it, get in.

Harold liked it when they drove past the cemetery work detail filing back to prison. The convicts had moved off the road and were looking back, waiting for the car. As they went by Harold raised one hand and waved. He said to Raymond, "Look at them poor boys. I believe they convicts."

8

"You know why they won't try to escape?" Mr. Manly said.

Bob Fisher stood at the desk and didn't say anything, because the answer was going to come from the little preacher anyway.

"Because they see the good in this. They realize this is their chance to become something."

"Running across a pasture field."

"You know what I mean."

"Take a man outside enough times," Fisher said, "he'll run for the hills."

"Not these two boys."

"Any two. They been outside every day for a week and they're smelling fresh air."

"Two weeks, and they can run three miles without stopping," Mr. Manly said. "Another couple of weeks I want to see them running five miles, maybe six."

"They'll run as long as it's easier than working."

Mr. Manly smiled a little. "I see you don't know them very well."

"I have known them all my life," Bob Fisher said.

"When running becomes harder than working, they'll figure a way to get out of it. They'll break each other's legs if they have to."

"All right, then I'll talk to them again. You can be present, Bob, and I'll prove to you you're wrong."

"I understand you write a weekly report to Mr. Rynning," Fisher said. "Have you told him what you're doing?"

"As a matter of fact, I have."

"You told him you got them running outside?"

"I told him I'm trying something out on two boys considered incorrigible, a program that combines spiritual teaching and physical exercise. He's made no mention to me what he thinks. But if you want to write to him, Bob, go right ahead."

"If it's all the same to you," Fisher said, "I want it on the record I didn't have nothing to do with this in any way at all."

Three miles wasn't so bad and it was easier to breathe at the end of the stretch. It didn't feel as if their lungs were burning any more. They would walk for a few minutes and run another mile and then walk again. Maybe they could do it again, run another mile before resting. But why do it if they didn't have to, if the guards didn't expect it? They would run a little way and when Raymond or Harold would call out they had to rest the car and would stop and wait for them.

"I think we could do it," Raymond said.

"Sure we could."

"Maybe run four, five miles at the start."

"We could do that too," Harold said, "but why would we want to?"

"I mean to see if we could do it."

"Man, we could run five miles right now if we wanted."

"I don't know."

"If we had something to run for. All I see it doing is getting us tired."

"It's better than laying adobes, or working on the rock pile."

"I believe you're right there," Harold said.

"Well," Raymond said, "we can try four miles, five miles at any time we want. What's the hurry?"

"What's the hurry," Harold said. "I wish that son of a bitch would give us a cigarette. Look at him sucking on it and blowing the smoke out. Man."

They were getting along all right with the guards, because the guards were finding out this was pretty good duty, driving around the countryside in a Ford Touring Car. Ride around for a few hours. Smoke any time they wanted. Put the canvas top up if it got too hot in the sun. The guards weren't dumb, though. They stayed away from trees and the riverbank, keeping to open range country once they had followed the railroad tracks out beyond town.

The idea of a train going by interested Harold. He pictured them running along the road where it was close to the tracks and the train coming up behind them out of the depot, not moving too fast. As the guards watched the train, Harold saw himself and Raymond break through the weeds to the gravel roadbed, run with the train and swing up on one of those iron-rung ladders they had on boxcars. Then the good part. The guards are watching the train and all of a sudden the guards see them on the boxcar—*waving to them.*

"Waving good-bye," Harold said to Raymond when they were resting one time and he told him about it.

Raymond was grinning. "They see the train going away, they don't know what to do."

"Oh, they take a couple of shots," Harold said. "But they so excited, man, they can't even hit the train."

"We're waving bye-bye."

"Yeah, while they shooting at us."

"It would be something, all right." Raymond had to wipe his eyes.

After a minute Harold said, "Where does the train go to?"

"I don't know. I guess different places."

"That's the trouble," Harold said. "You got to know where you going. You can't stay on the train. Sooner or later you got to get off and start running again."

"You think we could run five miles, uh?"

"If we wanted to," Harold said.

It was about a week later that Mr. Manly woke up in the middle of the night and said out loud in the bedroom, "All right, if you're going to keep worrying about it, why don't you see for yourself what they're doing?"

That's what he did the next day: hopped in the front seat of the Ford Touring Car and went along to watch the two boys do their road work.

It didn't bother the guard driving too much. He had less to say was all. But the guard with the Winchester yelled at Raymond and Harold more than he ever did before to come on, pick 'em up, keep closer to the car. Mr. Manly said the dust was probably bothering them. The guard said it was bothering him too, because he had to see them before he could watch them. He said you get a con outside you watch him every second.

Raymond and Harold ran three miles and saw Mr. Manly looking at his watch. Later on, when they were resting, he came over and squatted down in the grass with them.

"Three miles in twenty-five minutes," he said. "That's pretty good. You reckon you could cover five miles in an hour?"

"I don't think so," Raymond said. "It's not us, we want to do it. It's our legs."

"Well, wanting something is half of getting it," Mr. Manly said. "I mean if you want something bad enough."

"Sure, we want to do it."

"Why?"

"Why? Well, I guess because we got to do it."

"You just said you wanted to."

"Yeah, we like to run."

"And I'm asking you why." Mr. Manly waited a moment. "Somebody told me all you fellas want to do is get out of work."

"Who tole you that?"

"It doesn't matter who it was. You know what I told him? I told him he didn't know you boys very well. I told

149

him you were working harder now, running, than you ever worked in your life."

"That's right," Raymond said.

"Because you see a chance of doing something nobody else in the prison can do. Run twenty miles in a day."

Raymond said, "You want us to run twenty miles?"

"*You* want to run twenty miles. You're an Apache Indian, aren't you? And Harold's a Zulu. Well, by golly, an Apache Indian and a Zulu can run twenty miles, thirty miles a day, and there ain't a white man in this territory can say that."

"You want us to run twenty miles?" Raymond said again.

"I want you to start thinking of who you are, that's what I want. I want you to start thinking like warriors for a change instead of like convicts."

Raymond was watching him, nodding as he listened. He said, "Do these waryers think different than other people?"

"They think of who they are." An angry little edge came into Mr. Manly's tone. "They got pride in their tribe and their job, and everything they do is to make them better warriors—the way they live, the way they dress, the way they train to harden theirselves, the way they go without food or water to show their bodies their willpower is in charge here and, by golly, their bodies better do what they're told. Raymond, you say you're Apache Indian?"

"Yes, sir, that's right."

"Harold, you believe you're a Zulu?"

"Yes-suh, captain, a Zulu."

"Then prove it to me, both of you. Let me see how good you are."

As Mr. Manly got to his feet he glanced over at the guards, feeling a little funny now in the silence and wondering if they had been listening. Well, so what if they had? He was superintendent, wasn't he? And he answered right back, You're darn right.

"You boys get ready for some real training," he said now. "I'm taking you at your word."

Raymond waited until he walked away and had reached the car. "Who do you think tole him we're doing this to get out of work?"

"I don't know," Harold said. "Who do you think?"

"I think that son of a bitch Frank Shelby."

"Yeah," Harold said, "he'd do it, wouldn't he?"

On Visiting Day the mess-hall tables were placed in a single line, dividing the room down the middle. The visitors remained on one side and the convicts on the other. Friends and relatives could sit down facing each other if they found a place at the tables; but they couldn't touch, not even hands, and a visitor was not allowed to pass anything to a convict.

Frank Shelby always got a place at the tables and his visitor was always his brother, a slightly older and heavier brother, but used to taking orders from Frank.

Virgil Shelby said, "By May for sure."

"I don't want a month," Frank said. "I want a day."

"I'm telling you what I know. They're done building the place, they're doing something inside the walls now and they won't let anybody in."

"You can talk to a workman."

"I talked to plenty of workmen. They don't know anything."

"What about the railroad?"

"Same thing. Old boys in the saloon talk about moving the convicts, but they don't know when."

"Somebody knows."

"Maybe they don't. Frank, what are you worried about? Whatever the day is we're going to be ready. I've been over and across that rail line eight times—nine times now—and I know just where I'm going to take you off that train."

"You're talking too loud."

Virgil took time to look down the table both ways, at the convicts hunched over the tables shoulder to shoulder and their visitors crowded in on this side, everyone trying to talk naturally without being overheard. When Virgil looked at his brother again, he said, "What I want to know is how many?"

"Me. Junior, Soonzy, Joe Dean. Norma." Frank Shelby paused. "No, we don't need to take Norma."

"It's up to you."

"No, we don't need her."

"That's four. I want to know you're together, all in the same place, because once we hit that train there's going to be striped suits running all over the countryside."

"That might be all right."

"It could be. Give them some people to chase after. But it could mess things up too."

"Well, right now all I hear is you wondering what's going to happen. You come with more than that, or I live the next forty years in Florence, Arizona."

"I'm going to stay in Yuma a while, see what I can find out about the train. You need any money?" Virgil asked.

"If I have to buy some guards. I don't know, get me three, four hundred."

"I'll send it in with the stores. Anything else?"

"A good idea, buddy."

"Don't worry, Frank, we're going to get you out. I'll swear to it."

"Yeah, well, I'll see you."

"Next month," Virgil said. He turned to swing a leg over the bench, then looked at his brother again. "Something funny I seen coming here—these two convicts running behind a Ford automobile. What do you suppose they was doing, Frank?"

Shelby had to tear his pants nearly off to see Norma again. He ripped them down the in-seam from crotch to ankle and told the warehouse guard he'd caught them on some bailing wire and, man, it had almost fixed him good. The guard said to get another pair out of stores. Shelby said all right, and he'd leave his ripped pants at the tailor's on the way back. The guard knew what Shelby was up to; he accepted the sack of Bull Durham Shelby offered and played the game with him. It wasn't hurting anybody.

So he got his new pants and headed for the tailor shop. As soon as he was inside, Norma Davis came off the work table, where she was sitting smoking a cigarette, and went into the stock room. Shelby threw the ripped pants at the tailor, told Tacha to watch out the window for Bob Fisher, and followed Norma into the back room, closing the door behind him.

"He's not as sure of himself as he used to be," Tacha said. "He's worried."

The tailor was studying the ripped seam closely.

Tacha was looking out the window, at the colorless tone of the yard in sunlight: adobe and granite and black shadow lines in the glare. The brick detail was at work across the yard, but she couldn't hear them. She listened for sounds, out in the yard and in the room behind her, but there were none.

"They're quiet in there, uh?"

The tailor said nothing.

"You expect them to make sounds like animals, those two. That old turnkey makes sounds. God, like he's dying. Like somebody stuck a knife—" Tacha stopped.

"I don't know what you're talking about," the tailor said.

"I'm talking about Mr. Fisher, the turnkey, the sounds he makes when he's in her cell."

"And I don't want to know." The tailor kept his head low over his sewing machine.

"He sneaks in at night—"

"I said I don't want to hear about it."

"He hasn't been coming very long. Just the past few

weeks. Not every night either. He makes some excuse to go in there, like to fix the lantern or search the place for I don't know what. One time she say, 'Oh, I think there is a tarantula in here,' and the turnkey hurries in there to kill it. I want to say to him, knowing he's taking off his pants then, 'Hey, mister, that's a funny thing to kill a tarantula with.' "

"I'm not listening to you," the tailor said. "Not a word."

In the closeness of the stock room Shelby stepped back to rest his arm on one of the shelves. Watching Norma, he loosened his hat, setting it lightly on his forehead. "Goodness," he said, "I didn't even take off my hat, did I?"

Norma let her skirt fall. She smoothed it over her hips and began buttoning her blouse. "I feel like a mare, standing like that."

"Honey, you don't look like a mare. I believe you are about the trickiest thing I ever met."

"I know a few more ways."

"I bet you do, for a fact."

"That old man, he breathes through his nose right in your ear. Real loud, like he's having heart failure."

Shelby grinned. "That would be something. He has a stroke while he's in there with you."

"I'll tell you, he isn't any fun at all."

"You ain't loving him for the pleasure, sweetheart. You're supposed to be finding out things."

"He doesn't know yet when we're going."

"You asked him?"

"I said to him, 'I will sure be glad to get out of this place.' He said it wouldn't be much longer and I said, 'Oh, when are we leaving here?' He said he didn't know for sure, probably in a couple of months."

"We got to know the day," Shelby said.

"Well, if he don't know it he can't hardly tell me, can he?"

"Maybe he can find it out."

"From who?"

"I don't know. The superintendent, somebody."

"That little fella, he walks around, he looks like he's lost, can't find his mama."

"Well, mama, maybe you should talk to him."

"Get him to come to my cell."

"Jesus, you'd eat him up."

Norma giggled. "You say terrible things."

"I mean by the time you're through there wouldn't be nothing left of him."

"If *you're* through, you better get out of here."

"I talked to Virgil. He doesn't know anything either."

"Don't worry," Norma said. "One of us'll find out. I just want to be sure you take me along when the time comes."

Shelby gave her a nice little sad smile and shook his head slowly. "Sweetheart," he said, "how could I go anywhere without you?"

Good timing, Norma Davis believed, was one of the most important things in life. You had to think of the other person. You had to know his moods and reactions and know the right moment to spring little surprises.

You didn't want the person getting too excited and ruining everything before it was time.

That's why she brought Bob Fisher along for almost two months before she told him her secret.

It was strange; like instinct. One night, as she heard the key turning in the iron door of the cellblock, she knew it was Bob and, for some reason, she also knew she was going to tell him tonight. Though not right away.

First he had to go through his act. He had to look in at Tacha and ask her what was she doing, reading? Then he had to come over and see Norma in the bunk and look around the cell for a minute and ask if everything was all right. Norma was ready. She told him she had a terrible sore ankle and would he look at it and see if it was sprained or anything. She got him in there and then had to slow down and be patient while he actually, honest to God, looked at her ankle and said in a loud voice it looked all right to him. He whispered after that, getting out of his coat and into the bunk with her, but raising up every once in a while to look at the cell door.

Norma said, "What's the matter?"

"Tacha, she can hear everything."

"If she bothers you, why don't you put her some place else?"

"This is the women's block. There isn't any place else."

Norma got her hand inside his shirt and started fooling with the hair on his chest. "How does Tacha look to you?"

"Cut it out, it tickles," Fisher said. "What do you mean, how does she look?"

"I don't know, I don' think she looks so good. I hear her coughing at night."

"Listen, I only got a few minutes."

Norma handled the next part of it, making him believe he was driving her wild, and as he lay on the edge of the bunk breathing out of his nose, she told him her secret.

She said, "Guess what? I know somebody who's planning to escape."

That got him up and leaning over her again.

"Who?"

"I heard once," Norma said, "if you help the authorities here they'll help you."

"Who is it?"

"I heard of convicts who helped stop men trying to escape and got pardoned. Is that right?"

"It's happened."

"They were freed?"

"That's right."

"You think it might happen again?"

"It could. Who's going out?"

"Not out of here. From the train. You think if I found out all about it and told you I'd get a pardon?"

"I think you might," Fisher said. "I can't promise, but you'd have a good chance."

"It's Frank Shelby."

"That's what I thought."

"His brother Virgil's going to help him."

"Where do they jump the train?"

"Frank doesn't know yet, but soon as I find out I'll tell you."

"You promise?"

"Cross my heart."

"You're a sweet girl, Norma. You know that?"

She smiled at him in the dim glow of the lantern and said, "I try to be."

Another week passed before Bob Fisher thought of something else Norma had said.

He was in the tailor shop that day, just checking, not for any special reason. Tacha looked up at him and said, "Norma's not here."

"I can see that."

"She's at the toilet—if you're looking for her."

"I'm not looking for her," Fisher said.

He wasn't sure if Tacha was smiling then or not—like telling him she knew all about him. Little Mexican bitch, she had better not try to get smart with him.

It was then he thought of what Norma had said. About Tacha not looking so good. Coughing at night.

Hell, yes, Bob Fisher said to himself and wondered why he hadn't thought of it before. There was only one place around here to put anybody who was coughing sick. Over in the TB cellblock.

9

The guard, R. E. Baylis, was instructed to move the Mexican girl to the TB area after work, right before supper. It sounded easy enough.

But when he told Tacha she held back and didn't want to go. What for? Look at her. Did she look like she had TB? She wasn't even sick. R. E. Baylis told her to get her things, she was going over there and that's all there was to it. She asked him if Mr. Fisher had given the order, and when he said sure, Tacha said she thought so; she should have known he would do something like this. Goddamn-it, R. E. Baylis thought, he didn't have to explain anything to her. He did though. He said it must be they were sending her over there to help out—bring the lungers their food, get them their medicine. He said there were two boys in there supposed to be looking after the lungers, but nobody had seen much of them the past couple of months or so, what with all the running they were doing. They would go out early in the morning, just about the time it was getting light, and generally not get back until the afternoon. He said some of the guards were talking about them, how they had changed;

161

but he hadn't seen them in a while. Tacha only half listened to him. She wasn't interested in the two convicts, she was thinking about the TB cellblock and wondering what it would be like to live there. She remembered the two he was talking about; she knew them by sight. Though when she walked into the TB yard and saw them again, she did not recognize them immediately as the same two men.

R. E. Baylis got a close look at them and went to find Bob Fisher.

"She give you any trouble?" Fisher asked.

He sat at a table in the empty mess hall with a cup of coffee in front of him. The cooks were bringing in the serving pans and setting up for supper.

"No trouble once I got her there," R. E. Baylis said. "What I want to know is what the Indin and the nigger are doing?"

"I don't know anything about them and don't want to know. They're Mr. Manly's private convicts." Fisher held his cup close to his face and would lean in to sip at it.

"Haven't you seen them lately?"

"I see them go by once in a while, going out the gate."

"But you haven't been over there? You haven't seen them close?"

"Whatever he's got them doing isn't any of my business. I told him I don't want no part of it."

"You don't care what they're doing?"

"I got an inventory of equipment and stores have to be tallied before we ship out of here and that ain't very long away."

"You don't care if they made spears," R. E. Baylis said, "and they're throwing them at a board stuck in the ground?"

Bob Fisher started coughing and spilled some of his coffee down the front of his uniform.

Mr. Manly said, "Yes, I know they got spears. Made of bamboo fishing poles and brick-laying trowels stuck into one end for the point. If a man can use a trowel to work with all day, why can't he use one for exercise?"

"Because a spear is a weapon," Fisher said. "You can kill a man with it."

"Bob, you got some kind of stain there on your uniform."

"What I mean is you don't let convicts make *spears*."

"Why not, if they're for a good purpose?"

No, Bob Fisher said to himself—with R. E. Baylis standing next to him, listening to it all—this time, goddamn-it, don't let him mix you up. He said, "Mr. Manly, for some reason I seem to have trouble understanding you."

"What is it you don't understand, Bob?"

"Every time I come up here, it's like you and me are talking about two different things. I come in, I know what the rules are here and I know what I want to say. Then you begin talking and it's like we get onto something else."

"We look at a question from different points of view," Mr. Manly said. "That's all it is."

"All right, R. E. Baylis here says they got spears. I

163

haven't been over to see for myself. We was down-stairs—I don't know, something told me I should see you about it first."

"I'm glad you did."

"How long have they had 'em?"

"About two weeks. Bob, they run fourteen miles yesterday. Only stopped three times to rest."

"I don't see what that's got to do with the spears."

"Well, you said you wanted it to show in the record you're not having anything to do with this business. Isn't that right?"

"I want it to show I'm against their being taken outside."

"I haven't told you anything what's going on, have I?"

"I haven't asked neither."

"That's right. This is the first time you've mentioned those boys in over two months. You don't know what I'm teaching them, but you come in here and tell me they can't have spears."

"It's in the rules."

"It says in the rules they can't have spears for any purpose whatsoever?"

"It say a man found with a weapon is to be put under maximum security for no less than ten days."

"You mean put in the snake den."

"I sure do."

"You believe those two boys have been found with weapons?"

"When you make a spear out of a trowel, it becomes a weapon."

"But what if I was the one told them to make the spears?"

"I was afraid you might say that."

"As a matter of fact, I got them the fishing poles myself. Bought them in town."

"Bought them in town," Bob Fisher said. His head seemed to nod a little as he stared at Mr. Manly. "This here is what I meant before about not understanding some things. I would sure like to know why you want them to have spears?"

"Bob," Mr. Manly said, "that's the only way to learn, isn't it? Ask questions." He looked up past Fisher then, at the wall clock. "Say, it's about supper time already."

"Mr. Manly, I'll wait on supper if you'll explain them spears to me."

"I'll do better than that," Mr. Manly said, "I'll show you. First though we got to get us a pitcher of ice water."

"I'll even pass on that," Fisher said. "I'm not thirsty *or* hungry."

Mr. Manly gave him a patient, understanding grin. "The ice water isn't for us, Bob."

"No sir," Fisher said. He was nodding again, very slowly, solemnly. "I should've known better, shouldn't I?"

Tacha remembered them from months before wearing leg-irons and pushing the wheelbarrows. She remembered the Negro working without a shirt on and remembered thinking the other one tall for an Indian. She had never spoken to them or watched them for a definite reason. She had probably not been closer than fifty feet to either of them. But she was aware now of the striking change in their appearance and at first it gave her a strange, tense feeling. She was afraid of them.

The guard had looked as if he was afraid of them too, and maybe that was part of the strange feeling. He didn't tell her which cell was to be hers. He stared at the Indian and the Negro, who were across the sixty-foot yard by the wall, and then hurried away, leaving her here.

As soon as he was gone the tubercular convicts began talking to her. One of them asked if she had come to live with them. When she nodded he said she could bunk with him if she wanted. They laughed and another one said no, come on in his cell, he would show her a fine old time. She didn't like the way they stared at her. They sat in front of their cells on stools and a wooden bunk frame and looked as if they had been there a long time and seldom shaved or washed themselves.

She wasn't sure if the Indian and the Negro were watching her. The Indian was holding something that looked like a fishing pole. The Negro was standing by an upright board that was as tall as he was and seemed to be nailed to a post. Another of the poles was sticking out of the board. Neither of them was wearing a shirt; that was the first thing she noticed about them from across the yard.

They came over when she turned to look at the cells and one of the tubercular convicts told her again to come on, put her blanket and stuff in with his. Now, when she looked around, not knowing what to do, she saw them approaching.

She saw the Indian's hair, how long it was, covering his ears, and the striped red and black cloth he wore as a headband. She saw the Negro's mustache that curved around his mouth into a short beard and the cuts on his face, like knife scars, that slanted down from both of his cheekbones. This was when she was afraid of them, as they walked up to her.

"The cell on the end," Raymond said. "Why don't you take that one?"

She made herself hold his gaze. "Who else is in there, you?"

"Nobody else."

Harold said, "You got the TB?"

"I don't have it yet."

"You do something to Frank Shelby?"

"Maybe I did," she said, "I don't know."

"If you don't have the TB," Harold said, "you did something to somebody."

She began to feel less afraid already, talking to them, and yet she knew there was something different about their faces and the way they looked at her. "I think the turnkey, Mr. Fisher, did it," Tacha said, "so I wouldn't see him going in with Norma."

"I guess there are all kinds of things going on," Harold said. "They put you in here, it's not so bad. It was cold at night when we first come, colder than the big cellblock, but now it's all right." He glanced toward the tubercular convicts. "Don't worry about the scarecrows. They won't hurt you."

"They lock everybody in at night," Raymond said. "During the day one of them tries something, you can run."

That was a strange thing too: being afraid of them at first because of the way they looked, then hearing them say not to worry and feeling at ease with them, believing them.

Raymond said, "We fixed up that cell for you. It's like a new one."

She was inside unrolling her bedding when the guard returned with the superintendent and the turnkey, Mr. Fisher. She heard one of them say, "Harold, come out here," and she looked up to see them through the open doorway: the little man in the dark suit and two in guard uniforms, one of them, R. E. Baylis, holding a dented tin pitcher. The Indian was still in the yard, not far from them, but she didn't see the Negro. The superintendent was looking toward her cell now, squinting into the dim interior.

Mr. Manly wanted to keep an eye on Bob Fisher and watch his reactions, but seeing the woman distracted him.

"Who's that in there, Norma Davis?"

"The other one," Fisher said, "the Mexican."

"I didn't see any report on her being sick."

"She's working here. Your two boys run off, there's nobody to fetch things for the lungers."

Mr. Manly didn't like to look at the tubercular convicts; they gave him a creepy feeling, the way they sat there all day like lizards and never seemed to move. He gave them a glance and called again, "Harold, come on out here."

The Negro was buttoning a prison shirt as he appeared in the doorway. "You want me, captain?"

"Come over here, will you?"

Mr. Manly was watching Fisher now. The man's flat open-eyed expression tickled him: old Bob Fisher staring at Harold, then looking over at Raymond, then back at Harold again, trying to figure out the change that had come over them. The change was something more than just their appearance. It was something Mr. Manly felt, and he was pretty sure now Bob Fisher was feeling it too.

"What's the matter, Bob, ain't you ever seen an Apache or a Zulu before?"

"I seen Apaches."

"Then what're you staring at?"

Fisher looked over at Harold again. "What're them cuts on his face?"

"Tell him, Harold."

"They tribal marks, captain."

Fisher said, "What the hell tribe's a field nigger belong to?"

Harold touched his face, feeling the welts of scar tissue that were not yet completely healed. He said, "My tribe, captain."

"He cut his own face like that?"

Fisher kept staring at the Negro as Mr. Manly said, "He saw it in a Africa book I got—picture of a native with these marks like tattoos on his face. I didn't tell him

169

to do it, you understand. He just figured it would be all right, I guess. Isn't that so, Harold?"

"Yes-suh, captain."

"Same with Raymond. He figured if he's a full-blooded Apache Indian then he should let his hair grow and wear one of them bands."

"We come over here to look at spears," Fisher said.

Mr. Manly frowned, shaking his head. "Don't you see the connection yet? A spear is part of a warrior's get-up, like a tool is to a working man. Listen, I told you, didn't I, these boys can run fifteen miles in a day now and only stop a couple of times to rest."

"I thought it was fourteen miles," Fisher said.

"Fourteen, fifteen—here's the thing. They can run that far *and* go from morning to supper time without a drink of water, any time they want."

"A man will do that in the snake den if I make him." Bob Fisher wasn't backing off this time.

Mr. Manly wasn't letting go. "Inside," he said, "is different than running out in the hot sun. Listen, they each pour theirselves a cup of water in the morning and you know what they do? They see who can go all day without taking a drink or more than a couple of sips." He held his hand out to R. E. Baylis and said, "Let me have the pitcher." Then he looked at Raymond and Harold again. "Which of you won today?"

"I did," Raymond said.

"Let's see your cups."

Raymond went into his cell and was back in a moment with a tin cup in each hand. "He drank his. See, I got some left."

"Then you get the pitcher of ice water," Mr. Manly said. "And, Harold, you get to watch him drink it."

Raymond raised the pitcher and drank out of the side of it, not taking very much before lowering it again and holding it in front of him.

"See that?" Mr. Manly said. "He knows better than to gulp it down. One day Raymond wins, the next day Harold gets the ice water. I mean they can both do it any time they want."

"I would sure like to see them spears," Fisher said.

Mr. Manly asked Harold where they were and he said, "Over yonder by the wall, captain."

Tacha watched them cross the yard. The Negro waited for the Indian to put the pitcher on the ground and she noticed they gave each other a look as they fell in behind the little man in the dark suit and the two guards. They were over by the wall a few minutes talking while Mr. Fisher hefted one of the bamboo spears and felt the point of it with his finger. Then the superintendent took the spear from him and gave it to the Indian. The Negro picked up the other spear from against the wall and they came back this way, toward the cells, at least a dozen paces before turning around. Beyond them, the group moved away from the upright board. The Indian and the Negro faced the target for a moment, then stepped back several more feet, noticing Tacha now in the doorway of her cell.

She said, "You're going to hit that, way down there?"

"Not today," Raymond answered.

Everyone in the yard was watching them now. They raised the spears shoulder high, took aim with their outstretched left arms pointing, and threw them hard in a low arc, almost at the same moment. Both spears fell short and skidded along the ground past the board to stop at the base of the wall.

Raymond and Harold waited. In the group across the yard Mr. Manly seemed to be doing the talking, gesturing with his hands. He was facing Bob Fisher and did not look over this way. After a few minutes they left the yard, and now Mr. Manly, as he went through the gate last, looked over and waved.

"Well," Raymond said—he stooped to pick up the tin pitcher—"who wants some ice water?"

Within a few days Tacha realized that, since moving to the TB cellblock, she felt better—whether it made sense or not. Maybe part of the feeling was being outside most of the day and not bent over a sewing machine listening to Norma or trying to talk to the old man. Already that seemed like a long time ago. She was happier now. She even enjoyed being with the tubercular convicts and didn't mind the way they talked to her sometimes, saying she was a pretty good nurse though they would sure rather have her be something else. They needed to talk like men so she smiled and didn't take anything they said as an offense.

In the afternoon the Apache and the Zulu would come in through the gate, walking slowly, carrying their shirts. One of the tubercular convicts would yell over, asking how far they had run and one or the other would tell them twelve, fifteen, sixteen miles. They would drink the water in their cups. One of the convicts would fill the cups again from the bucket they kept in the shade. After drinking the second cup they would decide who the winner would be that day and pour just a little more water into his cup, leaving the other one empty. The TB convicts got a kick out of this and always laughed. Every day it was the same. They drank the water and then went into the cell to lie on their bunks. In less than an hour the TB convicts would be yelling for them to come out and start throwing their spears. They would get out their money or rolled cigarettes when the Apache and the Zulu appeared and, after letting them warm up a few minutes, at least two of the convicts would bet on every throw. Later on, after the work crews were in for the day, there would be convicts over from the main yard watching through the gate. None of them ever came into the TB yard. They were betting too and would yell at the Apache and the Zulu—calling them by those names—to hit the board, cut the son of a bitch dead center. Frank Shelby appeared at the gate only once. After that the convicts had to pay to watch and make bets. Soonzy, Junior, and Joe Dean were at the grillwork every day during free time.

Harold Jackson, the Zulu, walked over to the gate one time. He said, "How come we do all the work, you make all the money?"

Junior told him to get back over there and start throwing his goddamn spear or whatever it was.

Harold let the convicts get a good look at his face scars before he walked away. After the next throw, when

173

he and Raymond were pulling their spears out of the board, Harold said, "Somebody always telling you what to do, huh?"

"Every place you go," Raymond said.

They were good with the spears. Though when the convicts from the outside yard were at the gate watching they never threw from farther than thirty-five feet away, or tried to place the spears in a particular part of the board. If they wanted to, they could hit the board high or low at the same time.

It was Tacha who noticed their work shoes coming apart from the running and made moccasins for them, sewing them by hand—calf-high Apache moccasins she fashioned out of old leather water bags and feed sacks.

And it was Tacha who told Raymond he should put war paint on his face. He wasn't scarey enough looking.

"Where do you get war paint?" Raymond asked her. "At the store?"

"I think from berries."

"Well, I don't see no berries around here."

The next day she got iodine and a can of white enamel from the sick ward and, after supper, sat Raymond on a stool and painted a white streak across the bridge of his nose from cheekbone to cheekbone, and orange-red iodine stripes along the jawline to his chin.

Harold Jackson liked it, so Tacha painted a white stripe across his forehead and another one down between his eyes to the tip of his nose.

"Hey, we waryers now," Raymond said.

They looked at themselves in Tacha's hand mirror and both of them grinned. They were pretty mean-looking boys. Harold said, "Lady, what else do these waryers put on?"

Tacha said she guessed anything they wanted. She opened a little sack and gave Raymond two strands of turquoise beads, a string for around his neck and another string, doubled, for around his right arm, up high.

She asked Harold if he wanted a ring for his nose. He said no, thank you, lady, but remembered Mr. Manly talking about the Zulus putting chunks of sugar cane in their ear lobes and he let Tacha pierce one of his ears and attach a single gold earring. It looked good with the tribal scars and the mustache that curved into a short beard. "All I need me is a lion to spear," Harold said. He was Harold Jackson the Zulu, and he could feel it without looking in the mirror.

He didn't talk to Raymond about the feeling because he knew Raymond, in a way of his own, Raymond the Apache, had the same feeling. In front of the convicts who watched them throw spears or in front of the two guards who took them out to run, Harold could look at Raymond, their eyes would meet for a moment and each knew what the other was thinking. They didn't talk very much, even to each other. They walked slowly and seemed to expend no extra effort in their movements. They knew they could do something no other men in the prison could do—they could run all day and go without water—and it was part of the good feeling.

They began to put fresh paint on their faces almost every day, in the afternoon before they threw the spears.

10

The evening Junior and Joe Dean came for them they were sitting out in front of the cells with Tacha. It was after supper, just beginning to get dark. For a little while Tacha had been pretending to tell them their fortunes, using an old deck of cards and turning them up one at a time in the fading light. She told Harold she saw him sleeping under a banana tree with a big smile on his face. Sure, Cuba, Harold said. With the next card she saw him killing a lion with his spear and Harold was saying they didn't have no lions in Cuba, when Junior came up to them. Joe Dean stood over a little way with his hands in his pockets, watching.

"Frank wants to see you," Junior said. "Both of you." He took time to look at Tacha while he waited for them to get up. When neither of them moved he said, "You hear me? Frank wants you."

"What's he want?" Harold said.

"He's going to want me to kick your ass you don't get moving."

Raymond looked at Harold, and Harold looked at

Raymond. Finally they got up and followed them across the yard, though they moved so goddamn slow Worley Lewis, Jr. had to keep waiting for them with his hands on his hips, telling them to come on, *move*. They looked back once and saw Joe Dean still over by the cells. He seemed to be waiting for them to leave.

Soonzy was in the passageway of the main cellblock, standing in the light that was coming from No. 14. He motioned them inside.

They went into the cell, then stopped short. Frank Shelby was sitting on his throne reading a newspaper, hunched over before his own shadow on the back wall. He didn't look up; he made them wait several minutes before he finally rose, pulled up his pants and buckled his belt. Junior and Soonzy crowded the doorway behind them.

"Come closer to the light," Shelby said. He waited for them to move into the space between the bunks, to where the electric overhead light, with its tin shield, was almost directly above them.

"I want to ask you two something. I want to know how come you got your faces painted up like that."

They kept looking at him, but neither of them spoke.

"You going to tell me?"

"I don't know," Raymond said. "I guess it's hard to explain."

"Did anybody tell you to put it on?"

"No, we done it ourselves."

"Has this Mr. Manly seen it?"

"Yeah, but he didn't say nothing."

"You just figured it would be a good idea, uh?"

"I don't know," Raymond said. "We just done it, I guess."

"You want to look like a couple of circus clowns, is that it?"

"No, we didn't think of that."

"Maybe you want to look like a wild Indin," Shelby said, "and him, he wants to look like some kind of boogey-man native. Maybe that's it."

Raymond shrugged. "Maybe something like that. It's hard to explain."

"What does Mr. Jackson say about it?"

"If you know why we put it on," Harold said, "what are you asking us for?"

"Because it bothers me," Shelby answered. "I can't believe anybody would want to look like a nigger native. Even a nigger. Same as I can't believe anybody would want to look like a Wild West Show Indin 'less he was paid to do it. Somebody paying you, Raymond?"

"Nobody's paying us."

"See, Raymond, what bothers me—how can we learn people like you to act like white men if you're going to play you're savages? You see what I mean? You want to move back in this cellblock, but who do you think would want to live with you?"

"We're not white men," Raymond said.

"Jesus Christ, I know that. I'm saying if you want to live with white men then you got to try to act like white men. You start playing you're an Apache and a goddamn Zulu or something, that's the same as saying you

179

don't want to be a white man, and that's what bothers me something awful, when I see that going on."

There was a little space of silence before Harold said, "What do you want us to do?"

"We'll do it," Shelby said. "We're going to remind you how you're supposed to act."

Soonzy took Harold from behind with a fist in his hair and a forearm around his neck. He dragged Harold backward and as Raymond turned, Junior stepped in and hit Raymond with a belt wrapped around his fist. He had to hit Raymond again before he could get a good hold on him and pull him out of the cell. Joe Dean and a half-dozen convicts were waiting in the passageway. They got Raymond and Harold down on their backs on the cement. They sat on their legs and a convict stood on each of their outstretched hands and arms while another man got down and pulled their hair tight to keep them from moving their heads. Then Joe Dean took a brush and the can of enamel Tacha had got from the sick ward and painted both of their faces pure white.

When R. E. Baylis came through to lock up, Shelby told him to look at the goddamn mess out there, white paint all over the cement and dirty words painted on the wall. He said that nigger and his red nigger friend sneaked over and started messing up the place, but they caught the two and painted them as a lesson. Shelby said to R. E. Baylis goddamn-it, why didn't he throw them in the snake den so they would quit bothering people. R. E. Baylis said he would tell Bob Fisher.

The next morning after breakfast, Shelby came out of

the mess hall frowning in the sunlight and looking over the work details forming in the yard. He was walking toward the supply group when somebody called his name from behind. Bob Fisher was standing by the mess hall door: grim-looking tough old son of a bitch in his gray sack guard uniform. Shelby sure didn't want to, but he walked back to where the turnkey was standing.

"They don't know how to write even their names," Fisher said.

"Well"—Shelby took a moment to think—"maybe they got the paint for somebody else do to it."

"Joe Dean got the paint."

"Joe did that?"

"Him and Soonzy and Junior are going to clean it up before they go to work."

"Well, if they did it—"

"You're going to help them."

"Me? I'm on the supply detail. You know that."

"Or you can go with the quarry gang," Fisher said. "It don't make any difference to me."

"Quarry gang?" Shelby grinned to show Fisher he thought he was kidding. "I don't believe I ever done that kind of work."

"You'll do it if I say so."

"Listen, just because we painted those two boys up. We were teaching them a lesson, that's all. Christ, they go around here thinking they're something the way they fixed theirselves up—somebody had to teach them."

"I do the teaching here," Fisher said. "I'm teaching that to you right now."

Dumb, stone-face guard son of a bitch. Shelby said,

181

"Well," half-turning to look off thoughtfully toward the work groups waiting in the yard. "I hope those people don't get sore about this. You know how it is, how they listen to me and trust me. If they figure I'm getting treated unfair, they're liable to sit right down and not move from the yard, every one of them."

"If you believe that," Fisher said, "you better tell them I'll shoot the first man that sits down, and if they all sit down at once I'll shoot you."

Shelby waited. He didn't look at Bob Fisher; he kept his gaze on the convicts. After a moment he said, "You're kneeling on me for a reason, aren't you? You're waiting to see me make a terrible mistake."

"I believe you've already made it," Fisher said. He turned and went into the mess hall.

Scraping paint off cement was better than working in the quarry. It was hot in the passageway, but there was no sun beating down on them and they weren't breathing chalk dust. Shelby sat in his cell and let Junior, Soonzy, and Joe Dean do the work, until Bob Fisher came by. Fisher didn't say anything; he looked in at him and Shelby came out and picked up a trowel and started scraping. When Fisher was gone, Shelby sat back on his heels and said, "I'm going to bust me a guard, I'll tell you, if that man's anywhere near us when we leave."

The scraping stopped as he spoke, as Junior and Soonzy and Joe Dean waited to hear whatever he had to say.

"There is something bothering him," Shelby said. "He wants to nail me down. He could do it any time he feels like it, couldn't he? He could put me in the quarry or the snake den—that man could chain me to the wall. But he's waiting on something."

Joe Dean said, "Waiting on what?"

"I don't know. Unless he's telling me he knows what's going on. He could be saying, 'I got my eye on you, buddy. I'm waiting for you to make the wrong move.'"

"What could he know?" Joe Dean said. "We don't know anything ourselves."

"He could know we're thinking about it."

"He could be guessing."

"I mean," Shelby said, "he could *know*. Norma could have told him. She's the only other person who could."

Junior was frowning. "What would Norma want to tell him for?"

"Jesus Christ," Shelby said, "because she's Norma. She don't need a reason, she does what she feels like doing. Listen, she needs money she gets herself a forty-four and pours liquor into some crazy boy and they try and rob a goddamn *bank*. She's seeing Bob Fisher, and she's the only one could have told him anything."

"I say he's guessing," Joe Dean said. "The time's coming to move all these convicts, he's nervous at the thought of it, and starts guessing we're up to something."

"That could be right," Shelby said. "But the only way I can find out for sure is to talk to Norma." He was silent a moment. "I don't know. With old Bob watching every move I got to stay clear of the tailor shop."

"Why don't we bring her over here?" Junior said. "Right after supper everybody's in the yard. Shoot, we can get her in here, anywhere you want, no trouble."

"Hey, boy," Shelby grinned, "now you're talking."

Jesus, yes, what was he worrying about that old man turnkey for? He had to watch that and never worry out loud or raise his voice or lose his temper. He had to watch when little pissy-ant started to bother him. The Indin and the nigger had bothered him. It wasn't even important; but goddamn-it, it had bothered him and he had done something about it. See—but because of it Bob Fisher had come down on him and this was not anytime to get Bob Fisher nervous and watchful. Never trust a nervous person unless you've got a gun on him. That was a rule. And when you've got the gun on him shoot him or hit him with it, quick, but don't let him start crying and begging for his life and spilling the goddamn payroll all over the floor—the way it had happened in the paymaster's office at the Cornelia Mine near Ajo. They would have been out of there before the security guards arrived if he hadn't spilled the money. The paymaster would be alive if he hadn't spilled the money, and they wouldn't be in Yuma. There was such a thing as bad luck. Anything could happen during a holdup. But there had been five payroll and bank robberies before the Cornelia Mine job where no one had spilled the money or reached for a gun or walked in unexpectedly. They had been successful because they had kept calm and in control, and that was the way they had to do it again, to get out of here.

It had surely bothered him though—the way the Indin and the nigger had painted their faces.

* * *

Junior pushed through the mess-hall door behind Norma as she went out, and told her to go visit Tacha. That's how easy it was. When Norma got to the TB yard Joe Dean, standing by the gate, nodded toward the first cell. She saw Tacha sitting over a ways with the Indian and the Negro, and noticed there was something strange about them: they looked sick, with a gray pallor to their skin, even the Negro. Norma looked at Joe Dean and again he nodded toward the first cell.

Soonzy stepped out and walked past her as she approached the doorway. Shelby was waiting inside, standing with an arm on the upper bunk. He didn't grin or reach for her, he said, "How're you getting along with your boyfriend?"

"He still hasn't told me anything, if that's what you mean."

"I'm more interested in what you might have told him."

Norma smiled and seemed to relax. "You know, as I walked in here I thought you were a little tense about something."

"You haven't answered my question."

"What is it I might have told him?"

"Come on, Norma."

"I mean what's there to tell him? You don't have any plan you've told me about."

"I don't know," Shelby said, "it looks to me like you got your own plan."

"I ask him. Every time he comes in I bring it up. 'Honey, when are we going to get out of this awful place?' But he won't tell me anything."

"You were pretty sure one time you could squeeze it out of him."

"I don't believe he knows any more than we do."

"I'll tell you what," Shelby said. "I'll give you three more days to find out. You don't know anything by then, I don't see any reason to take you with us."

Norma took her time. She kept her eyes on Shelby, holding him and waiting a little, then stepped in close so that she was almost touching him with her body. She waited again before saying, quietly, "What're you being so mean for?"

Shelby said, "Man." He said, "Come on, Norma, if I want to put you on the bunk I'll put you on the bunk. Don't give me no sweetheart talk, all right? I want you to tell me if you're working something with that old man. Now hold on—I want you to keep looking right at me and tell me to my face yes or no—yes, 'I have told him,' or no, 'I have not told him.'"

Norma put on a frown now that brought her eyebrows together and gave her a nice hurt look.

"Frank, what do you want me to tell you?" She spaced the words to show how honest and truthful she was being, knowing that her upturned, frowning face was pretty nice and that her breasts were about an inch away from the upcurve of his belly.

She looked good all right, and if he put her down on the bunk she'd be something. But Frank Shelby was looking at a train and keeping calm, keeping his voice down, and he said, "Norma, if you don't find out anything in three days you don't leave this place."

It was Sunday, Visiting Day, that Mr. Manly decided he would make an announcement. He called Bob Fisher into his office to tell him, then thought better of it—Fisher would only object and argue—so he began talking about Raymond and Harold instead of his announcement.

"I'll tell you," Mr. Manly said, "I'm not so much interested in who did it as I am in *why* they did it. They got paint in their eyes, in their nose. They had to wash theirselves in gasoline and then they didn't get it all off."

"Well, there's no way of finding out now," Fisher said. "You ask them, there isn't anybody knows a thing."

"The men who did it know."

"Well, sure, the ones that did it."

"I'd like to know what a man thinks like would paint another person."

"They were painting theirselves before."

"I believe you see the difference, Bob."

"These are convicts," Fisher said. "They get mean they don't need a reason. It's the way they are."

"I'm thinking I better talk to them."

"But we don't know who done it."

"I mean talk to all of them. I want to talk to them about something else any way."

"About what?"

"Maybe I can make the person who did it come forward and admit it."

"Mister, if you believe that you don't know anything a-tall about convicts. You talked to Raymond and Harold, didn't you?"

"Yes, I did."

"And they won't even tell you who done it, will they?"

"I can't understand that."

"Because they're convicts. They know if they ever told you they'd get their heads beat against a cell wall. This is between them and the other convicts. If the convicts don't want them to paint up like savages then I believe we should stay out of it and let them settle it theirselves."

"But they've got rights—the two boys. What about them?"

"I don't know. I'm not talking about justice," Fisher said. "I'm talking about running a prison. If the convicts want these two to act a certain way or not act a certain way, we should keep out of it. It keeps them quiet and it don't cost us a cent. When you push against the whole convict body it had better be important and you had better be ready to shoot and kill people if they push back."

"I told them they could put on their paint if they wanted."

"Well, that's up to you," Fisher said. "Or it's up to them. I notice they been keeping their faces clean."

When Mr. Manly didn't speak right away, Fisher said, "If it's all right with you I want to get downstairs and keep an eye on things. It's Visiting Day."

Mr. Manly looked up. "That's right, it is. You know, I didn't tell you I been wanting to make an announcement. I believe I'll do it right now—sure, while some of them have their relatives here visiting." Mr. Manly's expression was bright and cheerful, as if he thought this was sure a swell idea.

* * *

"I don't know what you're doing," Shelby said, "but so far it isn't worth a rat's ass, is it?" He sat facing his brother, Virgil, who was leaning in against the table and looking directly at Frank to show he was sincere and doing everything he could to find out when the goddamn train was leaving. There were convicts and their visitors all the way down the line of tables that divided the mess hall: hunched over talking, filling the room with a low hum of voices.

"It ain't like looking up a schedule," Virgil said. "I believe this would be a special train, two or three cars probably. All right, I ask a lot of questions over at the railroad yard they begin wondering who I am, and somebody says hey, that's Virgil Shelby. His brother's up on the hill."

"That's Virgil Shelby," Frank said. "Jesus, do you believe people know who you are? You could be a mine engineer. You could be interested in hauling in equipment and you ask how they handle special trains. 'You ever put on a special run? You do? Like what kind?' Jesus, I mean you got to use your head and think for a change."

"Frank, I'm ready. I don't need to know more than a day ahead when you leave. I got me some good boys and, I'm telling you, we're going to *do* it."

"You're going to do what?"

"Get you off that train."

"How?"

"Stop it if we have to."

"How, Virgil?"

"Dynamite the track."

"Then what?"

"Then climb aboard."

"With the guards shooting at you?"

"You got to be doing something too," Virgil said. "Inside the train."

"I'm doing something right now. I'm seeing you don't know what you're talking about. And unless we know when the train leaves and where it stops, we're not going to be able to work out a plan. Do you see that, Virgil?"

"The train goes to Florence. We know that."

"Do we know if it stops anywhere? If it stops, Virgil, wouldn't that be the place to get on?"

"If it stops."

"That's right. That's what you got to find out. Because how are you going to know where to wait and when to wait if you don't know when the train's leaving here? Virgil, are you listening to me?"

His brother was looking past him at something. Shelby glanced over his shoulder. He turned then and kept looking as Mr. Manly, with Bob Fisher on the stairs at the far end of the mess hall, said, "May I have your attention a moment, please?"

Mr. Manly waited until the hum of voices trailed off and he saw the faces down the line of tables looking toward him: upturned, solemn faces, like people in church waiting for the sermon. Mr. Manly grinned. He always liked to open with a light touch.

He said, "I'm not going to make a speech, if any of you are worried about that. I just want to make a brief announcement while your relatives and loved ones are here. It will save the boys writing to tell you and I know some of them don't write as often as they should. By the way, I'm Everett Manly, the acting superintendent here in Mr. Rynning's absence." He paused to clear his throat.

"Now then—I am very pleased to announce that this will be the last Visiting Day at Yuma Territorial Prison. A week from tomorrow the first group of men will leave on the Southern Pacific for the new penitentiary at Florence, a fine new place I think you all are going to be very pleased with. Now you won't be able to tell your relatives or loved ones what day exactly you'll be leaving, but I promise you in three weeks everybody will be out of here and this place will open its doors forever and become a page in history. That's about all I can tell you right now for the present. However, if any of you have questions I will be glad to try and answer them."

Frank Shelby kept looking at the little man on the stairway. He said to himself, It's a trick. But the longer he stared at him—the little fellow standing up there waiting for questions—he knew Mr. Manly was telling the truth.

Virgil said, "Well, I guess that answers the question, doesn't it?"

Shelby didn't look at his brother. He was afraid he might lose his temper and hit Virgil in the mouth.

11

For three sacks of Mail Pouch, R. E. Baylis told Shelby the convicts would be sent out in groups of about forty at a time, going over every other day, it looked like, on the regular morning run.

R. E. Baylis even got Shelby a Southern Pacific schedule. Leave Yuma at 6:15 A.M. Pass through Sentinel at 8:56; no stop unless they needed coal or water. They'd stop at Gila at 9:51, where they'd be fed on the train; no one allowed off. They'd arrive in Phoenix at 2:40 P.M., switch the cars over to a Phoenix & Eastern train and arrive at Florence about 5:30 P.M. Bob Fisher planned to make the first run and the last one, the first one to see what the trip was like and the last one so he could lock up and officially hand over the keys.

Shelby asked R. E. Baylis if he would put him and his friends down for the first run, because they were sure anxious to get out of here. R. E. Baylis said he didn't know if it could be done, but maybe he could try to arrange it. Shelby gave him fifty dollars to try as hard as he could.

The guard told Bob Fisher about Shelby's request,

since Fisher would see the list anyway. Why the first train? Fisher wanted to know. What was the difference? R. E. Baylis asked. All the trains were going to the penitentiary. Fisher put himself in Shelby's place and thought about it a while. Maybe Shelby was anxious to leave, that could be a fact. But it wasn't the reason he wanted to be on the first train. It was so he would know exactly which train he'd be on, so he could tell somebody outside.

Fisher said all right, tell him he could go on the first train. But then, when the time came, they'd pull Shelby out of line and hold him for the last train. "I want him riding with me," Fisher said, "but not before I look over the route."

It bothered R. E. Baylis because Shelby had always treated him square and given him tobacco and things. He stopped by Shelby's cell that evening and said Lord, he could sure use that fifty dollars, but he would give it back. Bob Fisher was making them go on the last train. Shelby looked pretty disappointed. By God, he was big about it though. He let R. E. Baylis keep the fifty dollars anyway.

The next morning when he saw Junior and Soonzy and Joe Dean, Shelby grinned and said, "Boys, always trust a son of a bitch to be a son of a bitch. We're taking the last train."

All he had to do now was to get a letter of instructions to Virgil at the railroad hotel in Yuma. For a couple more sacks of Mail Pouch R. E. Baylis would probably deliver it personally.

* * *

Virgil Shelby and his three men arrived at Stout's Hotel in Gila on a Wednesday afternoon. Mr. Stout and a couple of Southern Pacific division men in the lobby got a kick out of these dudes who said they were heading south into the Saucedas to do some prospecting. All they had were bedrolls and rifles and a pack mule loaded with suitcases. The dudes were as serious about it though as they were ignorant. They bought four remount horses at the livery and two 50-pound cases of No. 1 dynamite at Tom Child's trading store, and on Thursday morning they rode out of Gila. They rode south two miles before turning west and doubling back to follow the train tracks.

They arrived in sight of the Southern Pacific water stop at Sentinel that evening and from a grove of trees studied the wooden buildings and frame structure that stood silently against a dark line of palo verdes. A water tank, a coaling shed, a section house and a little one-room station with a light showing in the window, that's all there was here.

As soon as Virgil saw the place he knew Frank was right again. Sometimes it made him mad when he sounded dumb in front of his brother. He had finished the sixth grade and Frank had gone on to the seventh or eighth. Maybe when Frank was looking at him, waiting, he would say the wrong thing or sound dumb; but Jesus, he had gone into places with a gun and put the gun in a man's face and got what he wanted. Frank didn't have to worry about him going in with a gun. He had not found out the important facts of the matter talking to the railroad people. He had not thought up the plan in all the time he'd had to do it. But he could sure do what Frank said in his letter. He had three good boys who would go with him for two hundred and fifty dollars each and bring the guns and know how to use them. These boys drank too much and got in fights, but they were the captains for this kind of work. Try and pick them. Try and get three fellows who had the nerve to stop a prison train and take off the people you wanted and do it right, without a lot of shooting and getting nervous and running off into the desert and hiding in a cave. He wished he had more like them, but these three said they could do the job and would put their guns on anybody for two hundred and fifty dollars.

He had a man named Howard Crowder who had worked for railroad lines in both the United States and Mexico, before he turned to holding up trains and spent ten years in Yuma.

He had an old hand named Dancey who had ridden with him and Frank before, and had been with them at the Cornelia Mine payroll robbery and had got away.

He had a third one named Billy Santos who had smuggled across the border whatever could be carried and was worth anything and knew all the trails and water holes south of here.

Five o'clock the next morning it still looked good and still looked easy as they walked into the little station at Sentinel with their suitcases and asked the S.P. man when the next eastbound train was coming through.

The S.P. man said 8:56 this morning, but that train

was not due to stop on account of it was carrying convicts some place.

Virgil asked him if there was anybody over in the section house. The S.P. man said no, he was alone. A crew
had gone out on the 8:45 to Gila the night before and
another crew was coming from Yuma sometime today.

Virgil looked over at Billy Santos. Billy went outside.
Howard Crowder and Dancey remained sitting on the
bench. The suitcases and bedrolls and rifles and two
cases of dynamite were on the floor by them. No, the
S.P. man behind the counter said, they couldn't take the
8:56, though they could get on the 8:48 this evening if
they wanted to hang around all day. But what will you
do with your horses? he said then. You rode in here,
didn't you?

Virgil was at the counter now. He nodded to the telegrapher's key on the desk behind the S.P. man and said,
"I hope you can work that thing, mister."

The S.P. man said, "Sure, I can work it. Else I
wouldn't be here."

"That's good," Virgil said. "It's better if they hear a
touch they are used to hearing."

The S.P. man gave Virgil a funny look, then let his
gaze shift over to the two men on the bench with all the
gear in front of them. They looked back at him; they
didn't move or say anything. The S.P. man was wondering if he should send a message to the division office at
Gila; tell them there were three dudes hanging around
here with rifles and dynamite and ask if they had been
seen in Gila the day before. He could probably get away

197

with it. How would these people know what he was saying? Just then the Mexican-looking one came back in, his eyes on the one standing by the counter, and shook his head.

Virgil said, "You all might as well get dressed."

The S.P. man watched them open the suitcases and take out gray and white convict suits. He watched them pull the pants and coats on over the clothes they were wearing and shove revolvers down into the pants and button the coats. One of them brought a double-barrel shotgun out of a suitcase in two pieces and sat down to fit the stock to the barrels. Watching them, the S.P. man said to Virgil Shelby, "Hey, what's going on? What is this?"

"This is how you stop a train," Virgil told him. "These are prisoners that escaped off the train that come through the day before yesterday."

"Nobody escaped," the S.P. man said.

Virgil nodded up and down. "Yes, they did, mister, and I'm the deputy sheriff of Maricopa County who's going to put them back on the train for Florence."

"If you're a deputy of this county," the S.P. man said, "then you're a new one."

"All right," Virgil said, "I'm a new one."

"If you're one at all."

Virgil pulled a .44 revolver from inside his coat and pointed it in the S.P. man's face. He said, "All you got to do is telegraph the Yuma depot at exactly six A.M. with a message for the prison superintendent, Mr. Everett Manly. You're going to say three escaped convicts are being held here at Sentinel and you request the train to stop and take them aboard. You also request an immediate answer and, mister," Virgil said, "I don't want you to send it one word different than I tell it to you. You understand?"

The S.P. man nodded. "I understand, but it ain't going to work. If three were missing at the head-count when they got to Florence, they would have already told Yuma about it."

"That's a fact," Virgil said. "That's why we had somebody wire the prison from Phoenix Wednesday night and report three missing." Virgil looked around then and said, "Howard?"

The one named Howard Crowder had a silver dollar in his hand. He began tapping the coin rapidly on the wooden bench next to him in sharp longs and shorts that were loud in the closed room. Virgil watched the expression on the S.P. man's face, the mouth come open a little.

"You understand that too?" Virgil asked him.

The S.P. man nodded.

"What did he say?"

"He said, 'Send correct message or you are a dead man.'"

"I'm happy you understand it," Virgil said.

The S.P. man watched the one named Dancey pry open a wooden case that was marked *High Explosives—Dangerous* and take out a paraffin-coated packet of dynamite sticks. He watched Dancey get out a coil of copper wire and detonator caps and work the wire gently into the open end of the cap and then crimp the end closed with his teeth. The Mexican-looking one was taking a box plunger out of a canvas bag. The S.P. man said to himself, My God, somebody is going to get killed and I am going to see it.

At six A.M. he sent the message to the depot at Yuma, where they would then be loading the convicts onto the train.

The Southern Pacific equipment that left Yuma that Friday morning was made up of a 4-4-0 locomotive, a baggage car, two day coaches for regular passengers (though only eleven people were aboard), another baggage car, and an old wooden coach from the Cannanea-Rio Yaqui-El Pacifico line. The last twenty-seven convicts to leave the prison were locked inside this coach along with Bob Fisher and three armed guards. Behind, bringing up the rear, was a caboose that carried Mr. Manly and three more guards.

Bob Fisher had personally made up the list of prisoners for this last run to Florence: only twenty-seven, including Frank Shelby and his bunch. Most of the others were short-term prisoners and trusties who wouldn't be expected to make trouble. A small, semi-harmless group which, Bob Fisher believed, would make it easy for him to keep an eye on Shelby. Also aboard were the TB convicts, the two women and Harold Jackson and Raymond San Carlos.

Harold and Raymond were near the rear of the coach. The only ones behind them were Bob Fisher and the guards. Ahead of them were the TB convicts, then two rows of empty seats, then the rest of the prisoners scattered along both sides of the aisle in the back-to-back straw seats. The two women were in the front of the coach. The doors at both ends were padlocked. The windows were glass, but they were not made to open.

Before the train was five minutes out of Yuma every convict in the coach knew they were going to stop in Sentinel to pick up three men who had escaped on Wednesday and had been recaptured the next day. There was a lot of talk about who the three were.

Bob Fisher didn't say a word. He sat patiently waiting for the train to reach Sentinel, thinking about the message they had received Wednesday evening: *Three convicts missing on arrival Phoenix. Local and county authorities alerted. Signed, Sheriff, Maricopa County.* What bothered Fisher, there had been no information sent from Florence, nothing from Mr. Rynning, no further word from anybody until the wire was received at the depot this morning. Mr. Manly had wired back they would stop for the prisoners and Bob Fisher had not said a word to anybody since. Something wasn't right and he had to think it through.

About 7:30 A.M., halfway to Sentinel, Fisher said to the guard sitting next to him, "Put your gun on Frank Shelby and don't move it till we get to Florence."

Harold Jackson, next to the window, looked out at the flat desert country that stretched to distant dark mounds, mountains that would take a day to reach on foot, maybe half a day if a man was to run. But a mountain was nothing to run to. There was nothing out there but sky and rocks and desert growth that looked as if it would never die, but offered a man no hope of life. It was the same land he had looked at a few months before, going in the other direction, sitting in the same up-

201

right straw seat handcuffed to a sheriff's man. The Indian sitting next to him now nudged his arm and Harold looked up.

The Davis woman was coming down the aisle from the front of the coach. She passed them and a moment later Harold heard the door to the toilet open and close. Looking out the window again, Harold said, "What's out there, that way?"

"Mexico," Raymond answered. "Across the desert and the mountain, and if you can find water, Mexico."

"You know where the water is?"

"First twenty-five, thirty miles there isn't any."

"What about after that?"

"I know some places."

"You could find them?"

"I'm not going through the window if that's what you're thinking about."

"The train's going to stop in Sentinel."

"They open the door to put people on," Raymond said. "They ain't letting anybody off."

"We don't know what they going to do," Harold said, "till we get there." He heard the woman come out of the toilet compartment and waited for her to walk past.

She didn't appear. Harold turned to look out the window across the aisle. Over his shoulder he could see the Davis woman standing by Bob Fisher's seat. She was saying something but keeping her voice down and he couldn't make out the words. He heard Fisher though. Fisher said, "Is that right?" The woman said something else and Fisher said, "If you don't know where what's the good of telling me? How are you helping? Anybody could say what you're saying and if it turns out right try to get credit. But you haven't told me nothing yet."

"All right," Norma Davis said. "It's going to be at Sentinel."

"You could be guessing, for all I know."

"Take my word," the woman said.

Bob Fisher didn't say anything for a while. The train swayed and clicked along the tracks and there was no sound behind Harold Jackson. He glanced over his shoulder. Fisher was getting up, handing his revolver to the guard sitting across the aisle. Then he was past Harold, walking up the aisle and holding the woman by the arm to move her along ahead of him.

Frank Shelby looked up as they stopped at his seat. He was sitting with Junior; Soonzy and Joe Dean were facing them.

"This lady says you're going to try to escape," Fisher said to Shelby. "What do you think about that?"

Shelby's shoulders and head swayed slightly with the motion of the train. He looked up at Fisher and Norma, looking from one to the other before he said, "If I haven't told her any such thing, how would she know?"

"She says you're getting off at Sentinel."

"Well, if she tells me how I'm going to do it and it sounds good, I might try it." Shelby grinned a little. "Do you believe her?"

"I believe she might be telling a story," Fisher said,

"but I also believe it might be true. That's why I've got a gun pointed at your head till we get to Florence. Do you understand me?"

"I sure do." Shelby nodded, looking straight up at Bob Fisher. He said then, "Do you mind if I have a talk with Norma? I'd like to know why she's making up stories."

"She's all yours," Fisher said.

Harold nudged Raymond. They watched Fisher coming back down the aisle. Beyond him they saw Junior get up to give the Davis woman his seat. Tacha was turned around watching. She moved over close to the window as Junior approached her and sat down.

Behind Harold and Raymond one of the guards said, "You letting the woman sit with the men?"

"They're all the same as far as I can see," Fisher answered. "All convicts."

Virgil Shelby, holding a shotgun across his arm, was out on the platform when the train came into sight. He heard it and saw its smoke first, then spotted the locomotive way down the tracks. This was the worst part, right now, seeing the train getting bigger and bigger and seeing the steam blowing out with the screeching sound of the brakes. The locomotive was rolling slowly as it came past the coaling shed and the water tower, easing into the station, rolling past the platform now hissing steam, the engine and the baggage cars and the two coaches with the half-dozen faces in the windows looking out at him. He could feel those people staring at him, wondering who he was. Virgil didn't look back at them. He kept his eyes on the last coach and caboose and saw them jerk to a stop before reaching the platform—out on open ground just this side of the water tower.

"Come on out," Virgil said to the station house.

Howard Crowder and Dancey and Billy Santos came out into the sunlight through the open door. Their hands were behind their backs, as though they might have been tied. Virgil moved them out of the doorway, down to the end of the platform and stood them against the wall of the building: three convicts waiting to be put aboard a prison train, tired-looking, beaten, their hat brims pulled down against the bright morning glare.

Virgil watched Bob Fisher, followed by another guard with a rifle come down the step-rungs at the far end of the prison coach. Two more guards with rifles were coming along the side of the caboose and somebody else was in the caboose window: a man wearing glasses who was sticking his head out and saying something to the two guards who had come out of the prison coach.

Bob Fisher didn't look around at Mr. Manly in the caboose window. He kept his gaze on the three convicts and the man with the shotgun. He called out, "What're the names of those men you got?"

"I'm just delivering these people," Virgil called back. "I wasn't introduced to them."

Bob Fisher and the guard with him and the two guards from the caboose came on past the prison coach but stopped before they reached the platform.

"You the only one guarding them?" Fisher asked.

"Yes, sir, I'm the one found them, I'm the one brought them in."

"I've seen you some place," Fisher said.

"Sure, delivering a prisoner. About a year ago."

"Where's the station man at?"

"He's inside."

"Call him out."

"I reckon he heard you." Virgil looked over his shoulder as the S.P. man appeared in the doorway. "There he is. Hey, listen, you want these three boys or don't you? I been watching them all night, I'm tired."

"I want to know who they are," Fisher said. "If you're not going to tell me, I want them to call out their names."

There was silence. Virgil knew the time had come and he had to put the shotgun on Fisher and fill up the silence and get this thing done right now, or else drop the gun and forget the whole thing. No more than eight seconds passed in the silence, though it seemed like eight minutes to Virgil. Bob Fisher's hand went inside his coat and Virgil didn't have to think about it any more. He heard glass shatter as somebody kicked through a window in the prison coach. Bob Fisher drew a revolver, half turning toward the prison coach at the same time, but not turning quickly enough as Virgil put the shotgun on him and gave him a load point-blank in the side of the chest. And as the guards saw Fisher go down and were raising their rifles the three men in convict clothes brought their revolvers from behind their backs and fired as fast as they could swing their guns from one gray suit to another. All three guards were dropped where they stood, though one of them, on his knees, shot Billy Santos through the head before Virgil could get his shotgun on the man and finish him with the second load.

A rifle came out the caboose window and a barrel smashed the glass of a window in the prison coach, but it was too late. Virgil was pressed close to the side of the baggage car, out of the line of fire, and the two men in prison clothes had the S.P. man and were using him for a shield as they backed into the station house.

Virgil could look directly across the platform to the open doorway. He took time to reload the shotgun. He looked up and down the length of the train, then over at the doorway again.

"Hey, Dancey," Virgil called over, "send that train man out with the dynamite."

He had to wait a little bit before the S.P. man appeared in the doorway, straining to hold the fifty-pound case in his arms, having trouble with the dead weight, or else terrified of what he was holding.

"Walk down to the end of the platform with it," Virgil told him, "so they can see what you got. When you come back, walk up by that first passenger coach. Where everybody's looking out the window."

Jesus, the man could hardly take a step he was so scared of dropping the case. When he was down at the end of the platform, the copper wire trailing behind him and leading into the station. Virgil stepped away from the baggage car and called out, "Hey, you guards! You hear me? Throw out your guns and come out with your hands in the air, or we're going to put dynamite under a passenger coach and blow everybody clear to hell. You hear me?"

They heard him.

Mr. Manly and the three guards who were left came out to stand by the caboose. The prisoners began to yell and break the windows on both sides of the coach, but they quieted down when Frank Shelby and his three boys walked off the train and wouldn't let anybody else follow.

They are going to shoot us, Mr. Manly said to himself. He saw Frank Shelby looking toward them. Then Frank was looking at the dead guards and at Bob Fisher in particular. "I wish you hadn't of killed him," he heard Shelby say.

"I had to," the man with the shotgun said.

And then Shelby said, "I wanted to do it."

Junior said that if he hadn't kicked out the window they might still be in there. That was all they said for a while that Mr. Manly heard. Shelby and his three convict friends went into the station house. They came out a few minutes later wearing work clothes and might have been ranch hands for all anybody would know to look at them.

Mr. Manly didn't see who it was that placed the case of dynamite at the front end of the train, under the cowcatcher, but saw one of them playing out the wire back along the platform and around the off side of the station house. Standing on the platform, Frank Shelby and the one with the shotgun seemed to be in a serious conversation. Then Frank said something to Junior, who boarded the train again and brought out Norma Davis. Mr. Manly could see she was frightened, as if afraid they were going to shoot her or do something to her. Junior and Joe Dean took her into the station house. Frank Shelby came over then. Mr. Manly expected him to draw a gun.

"Four of us are leaving," Shelby said. "You can have the rest."

"What about the woman?"

"I mean five of us. Norma's going along."

"You're not going to harm her, are you?" Shelby kept staring at him, and Mr. Manly couldn't think straight. All he could say was, "I hope you know that what you're doing is wrong, an offense against Almighty God as well as your fellowman."

"Jesus Christ," Shelby said, and walked away.

Lord, help me, Mr. Manly said, and called out, "Frank, listen to me."

But Shelby didn't look back. The platform was deserted now except for the Mexican-looking man who lay dead with his arm hanging over the edge. They were mounting horses on the other side of the station. Mr. Manly could hear the horses. Then, from where he stood, he could see several of the horses past the corner of the building. He saw Junior stand in his stirrups to reach the telegraph wire at the edge of the roof and cut it with a knife. Another man was on the ground, stooped over a wooden box. Shelby nodded to him and kicked his horse, heading out into the open desert, away from the station. As the rest of them followed, raising a thin dust cloud, the man on the ground pushed down on the box.

The dynamite charge raised the front end of the locomotive off the track, derailed the first baggage car and sent the coaches slamming back against each other, twisting the couplings and tearing loose the end car, rolling it a hundred feet down the track. Mr. Manly dropped flat with the awful, ear-splitting sound of the explosion. He wasn't sure if he threw himself down or was knocked down by the concussion. When he opened his eyes there was dirt in his mouth, his head throbbed as if he had been hit with a hammer, and for a minute or so he could see nothing but smoke or dust or steam from the engine, a cloud that enveloped the station and lay heavily over the platform.

He heard men's voices. He was aware of one of the guards lying close to him and looked to see if the man was hurt. The guard was pushing himself up, shaking his head. Mr. Manly got quickly to his feet and looked around. The caboose was no longer behind him; it was down the track and the prison coach was only a few feet away where the convicts were coming out, coughing and waving at the smoke with their hands. Mr. Manly called out, "Is anybody hurt?"

No one answered him directly. The convicts were standing around; they seemed dazed. No one was attempting to run away. He saw one of the guards with a rifle now on the platform, holding the gun on the prisoners, who were paying no attention to him. At the other end of the platform there were a few people from the passenger coach. They stood looking at the locomotive that was shooting white steam and stood leaning awkwardly toward the platform, as if it might fall over any minute.

He wanted to be doing something. He had to be doing something. Five prisoners gone, four guards dead, a train blown up, telegraph line cut, no idea when help would come or where to go from here. He could hear Mr. Rynning saying, "You let them do all that? Man, this is your responsibility and you'll answer for it."

"Captain, you want us to follow them?"

Mr. Manly turned, not recognizing the voice at first. Harold Jackson, the Zulu, was standing next to him.

"What? I'm sorry, I didn't hear you."

"I said, you want us to follow them? Me and Raymond."

Mr. Manly perked up. "There are horses here?"

"No-suh, man say the nearest horses are at Gila. That's most of a day's ride."

"Then how would you expect to follow them?"

"We run, captain."

"There are eight of them—on horses."

"We don't mean to fight them, captain. We mean maybe we can follow them and see which way they go. Then when you get some help, you know, maybe we can tell this help where they went."

"They'll be thirty miles away before dark."

"So will we, captain."

"Follow them on foot—"

"Yes-suh, only we would have to go right now. Captain, they going to run those horses at first to get some distance and we would have to run the first five, six miles, no stopping, to keep their dust in sight. Raymond say it's all flat and open, no water. Just some little bushes. We don't have to follow them all day. We see where they going and get back here at dark."

Mr. Manly was frowning, looking around because, Lord, there was too much to think about at one time. He said, "I can't send convicts to chase after convicts. My God."

"They do it in Florida, captain. Trusties handle the dogs. I seen it."

"I have to get the telegraph wire fixed, that's the main thing."

"I hear the train man say they busted his key, he don't know if he can fix it," Harold Jackson said. "You going to sit here till tonight before anybody come—while Frank Shelby and them are making distance. But if me and the Apache follow them we can leave signs."

Mr. Manly noticed Raymond San Carlos now behind Harold. Raymond was nodding. "Sure," he said, "we can leave pieces of our clothes for them to follow if you give us something else to wear. Maybe you should give us some guns too, in case we get close to them, or for firing signals."

"I can't do that," Mr. Manly said. "No, I can't give you guns."

"How about our spears then?" Raymond said. "We get hungry we could use the spears maybe to stick something."

"The spears might be all right." Mr. Manly nodded.

"Spears and two canteens of water," Raymond said. "And the other clothes. Some people see us they won't think we're convicts running away."

"Pair of pants and a shirt," Mr. Manly said.

"And a couple of blankets. In case we don't get back before dark and we got to sleep outside. We can get our bedrolls and the spears," Raymond said. "They're with all the baggage in that car we loaded."

"You'd try to be back before dark?"

"Yes, sir, we don't like to sleep outside if we don't have to."

"Well," Mr. Manly said. He paused. He was trying to think of an alternative. He didn't believe that sending these two out would do any good. He pictured them coming back at dusk and sinking to the ground exhausted. But at least it would be doing something—now. Mr. Rynning or somebody would ask him, What did you do? And he'd say, I sent trackers out after them. I got these two boys that are runners. He said, "Well, find your stuff and get started. I'll tell the guards."

They left the water stop at Sentinel running almost due south. They ran several hundred yards before looking back to see the smoke still hanging in a dull cloud over the buildings and the palo verde trees. They ran for another half-mile or so, loping easily and not speaking, carrying their spears and their new guard-gray pants and shirts wrapped in their blanket rolls. They ran until they reached a gradual rise and ran down the other side to find themselves in a shallow wash, out of sight of the water stop.

They looked at each other now. Harold grinned and Raymond grinned. They sat down on the bank of the wash and began laughing, until soon both of them had tears in their eyes.

12

Harold said, "What way do we go?"

Raymond got up on the bank of the dry wash and stood looking out at the desert that was a flat burned-out waste as far as they could see. There were patches of dusty scrub growth, but no cactus or trees from here to the dark rise of the mountains to the south.

"That way," Raymond said. "To the Crater Mountains and down to the Little Ajos. Two days we come to Ajo, the town, steal some horses, go on south to Bates Well. The next day we come to Quitobaquito, a little water-hole village, and cross the border. After that, I don't know."

"Three days, uh?"

"Without horses."

"Frank Shelby, he going the same way?"

"He could go to Clarkstown instead of Ajo. They near each other. One the white man's town, the other the Mexican town."

"But he's going the same way we are."

"There isn't no other way south from here."

"I'd like to get him in front of me one minute," Harold said.

"Man," Raymond said, "you would have to move fast to get him first."

"Maybe we run into him sometime."

"Only if we run," Raymond said.

Harold was silent a moment. "If we did, we'd get out of here quicker, wouldn't we? If we run."

"Sure, maybe save a day. If we're any good."

"You think we couldn't run to those mountains?"

"Sure we could, we wanted to."

"Is there water?"

"There used to be."

"Then that's probably where he's heading to camp tonight, uh? What do you think?"

"He's got to go that way. He might as well."

"We was to get there tonight," Harold said, "we might run into him."

"We might run into all of them."

"Not if we saw them first. Waited for him to get alone."

Raymond grinned. "Play with him a little."

"Man, that would be good, wouldn't it?" Harold said. "Scare him some."

"Scare hell out of him."

"Paint his face," Harold said. He began to smile thinking about it.

"Take his clothes. Paint him all over."

"Now you talking. You got any?"

"I brought some iodine and a little bottle of white.

Listen," Raymond said, "we're going that way. Why don't we take a little run and see how Frank's doing?"

Harold stood up. When they had tied their blanket rolls across one shoulder and picked up their spears, the Apache and the Zulu began their run across the southern Arizona desert.

They ran ten miles in the furnace heat of sand and rock and dry, white-crusted playas and didn't break their stride until the sun was directly overhead. They walked a mile and ran another mile before they stopped to rest and allowed themselves a drink of water from the canteens, a short drink and then a mouthful they held in their mouths while they screwed closed the canteens and hung them over their shoulders again. They rested fifteen minutes and before the tiredness could creep in to stiffen their legs they stood up without a word and started off again toward the mountains.

For a mile or so they would be aware of their running. Then, in time, they would become lost in the monotonous stride of their pace, running, but each somewhere else in his mind, seeing cool mountain pastures or palm trees or thinking of nothing at all, running and hearing themselves sucking the heated air in and letting it out, but not feeling the agony of running. They had learned to do this in the past months, to detach themselves and be inside or outside the running man but not part of him for long minutes at a time. When they broke stride they would always walk and sometimes run again before resting. At times they felt they were getting no closer to the mountains, though finally the slopes began to take shape, changing from a dark mass to dun-colored slopes and shadowed contours. At mid-afternoon they saw the first trace of dust rising in the distance. Both of them saw it and they kept their eyes on the wispy, moving cloud that would rise and vanish against the sky. The dust was something good to watch and seeing it was better than stretching out in the grass and going to sleep. It meant Frank Shelby was only a few miles ahead of them.

They came to the arroyo in the shadowed foothills of the Crater Mountains a little after five o'clock. There was good brush cover here and a natural road that would take them up into high country. They would camp above Shelby if they could and watch him, Ray-mond said, but first he had to go out and find the son of a bitch. You rest, he told Harold, and the Zulu gave him a deadpan look and stared at him until he was gone. Harold sat back against the cool, shaded wall of the gul-ley. He wouldn't let himself go to sleep though. He kept his eyes open and waited for the Apache, listening and not moving, letting the tight weariness ease out of his body. By the time Raymond returned the arroyo was dark. The only light they could see were sun reflections on the high peaks above them.

"They're in some trees," Raymond said, "about a half-mile from here. Taking it easy, they even got a fire."

"All of them there?"

"I count eight, eight horses."

"Can we get close?"

"Right above them. Frank's put two men up in the rocks—they can see all around the camp."

"What do you think?" Harold said.

"I think we should take the two in the rocks. See what Frank does in the morning when nobody's there."

The grin spread over Harold's face. That sounded pretty good.

They slept for a few hours and when they woke up it was night. Harold touched Raymond. The Indian sat up without making a sound. He opened a canvas bag and took out the small bottles of iodine and white paint and they began to get ready.

There was no sun yet on this side of the mountain, still cold dark in the early morning when Virgil Shelby came down out of the rocks and crossed the open slope to the trees. He could make out his brother and the woman by the fire. He could hear the horses and knew Frank's men were saddling them and gathering up their gear.

Frank and the woman looked up as Virgil approached, and Frank said, "They coming?"

"I don't know. I didn't see them."

"What do you mean you didn't see them?"

"They weren't up there."

Frank Shelby got up off the ground. He dumped his coffee as he walked to the edge of the trees to look up at the tumbled rocks and the escarpment that rose steeply against the sky.

"They're asleep somewhere," he said. "You must've looked the wrong places."

"I looked all over up there."

"They're asleep," Shelby said. "Go on up there and look again."

When Virgil came back the second time Frank said, Jesus Christ, what good are you? And sent Junior and Joe Dean up into the rocks. When they came down he went up himself to have a look and was still up there as the sunlight began to spread over the slope and they could feel the heat of day coming down on them.

"There's no sign of anything," Virgil said. "There's no sign they were even here."

"I put them here," Frank Shelby said. "One right where you're standing, Dancey over about a hundred feet. I put them here myself."

"Well, they're not here now," Virgil said.

"Jesus Christ, I know that." Frank looked over at Junior and Soonzy. "You counted the horses?"

"We'd a-heard them taking horses."

"I asked if you counted them!"

"Christ, we got them saddled. I don't have to count them."

"Then they walked away," Frank Shelby said, his tone quieter now.

Virgil shook his head. "I hadn't paid them yet."

"They walked away," Shelby said again. "I don't know why, but they did."

"Can you see Dancey walking off into the mountains?" Virgil said. "I'm telling you I hadn't *paid* them."

"There's nothing up there could have carried them off. No animal, no man. There is no sign they did anything but walk away," Shelby said, "and that's the way we're going to leave it."

He said no more until they were down in the trees again, ready to ride out. Nobody said anything.

Then Frank told Joe Dean he was to ride ahead of them like a point man. Virgil, he said, was to stay closer in the hills and ride swing, though he would also be ahead of them looking for natural trails.

"Looking for trails," Virgil said. "If you believe those two men walked off, then what is it that's tightening up your hind end?"

"You're older than me," Frank said, "but no bigger, and I will sure close your mouth if you want it done."

"Jesus, can't you take some kidding?"

"Not from you," his brother said.

They were in a high meadow that had taken more than an hour to reach, at least a thousand feet above Shelby's camp. Dancey and Howard Crowder sat on the ground close to each other. The Apache and the Zulu stood off from them leaning on their spears, their blankets laid over their shoulders as they waited for the sun to spread across the field. They would be leaving in a few minutes. They planned to get out ahead of Shelby and be waiting for him. These two, Dancey and Crowder, they would leave here. They had taken their revolvers and gun belts, the only things they wanted from them.

"They're going to kill us," Dancey whispered.

Howard Crowder told him for God sake to keep quiet, they'd hear him.

They had been in the meadow most of the night, brought here after each had been sitting in the rocks, drowsing, and had felt the spear point at the back of his neck. They hadn't got a good look at the two yet. They believed both were Indians—even though there were no

Indians around here, and no Indians had carried spears in fifty years. Then they would have to be loco Indians escaped from an asylum or kicked out of their village. That's what they were. That's why Dancey believed they were going to kill him and Howard.

Finally, in the morning light, when the Zulu walked over to them and Dancey got a close look at his face—God Almighty, with the paint and the scars and the short pointed beard and the earring—he closed his eyes and expected to feel the spear in his chest any second.

Harold said, "You two wait here till after we're gone."

Dancey opened his eyes and Howard Crowder said, "What?"

"We're going to leave, then you can find your way out of here."

Howard Crowder said, "But we don't know where we are."

"You up on a mountain."

"How do we get down?"

"You look around for a while you find a trail. By that time your friends will be gone without you, so you might as well go home." Howard started to turn away.

"Wait a minute," Howard Crowder said. "We don't have horses, we don't have any food or water. How are we supposed to get across the desert?"

"It's up to you," Harold said. "Walk if you want or stay here and die, it's up to you."

"We didn't do nothing to you," Dancey said.

Harold looked at him. "That's why we haven't killed you."

"Then what do you want us for?"

"We don't want you," Harold said. "We want Frank Shelby."

Virgil rejoined the group at noon to report he hadn't seen a thing, not any natural trail either that would save them time. They were into the foothills of the Little Ajos and he sure wished Billy Santos had not got shot in the head in the train station, because Billy would have had them to Clarkstown by now. They would be sitting at a table with cold beer and fried meat instead of squatting on the ground eating hash out of a can. He asked if he should stay with the group now. Norma Davis looked pretty good even if she was kind of sweaty and dirty; she was built and had nice long hair. He wouldn't mind riding with her a while and maybe arranging something for that night.

Frank, it looked like, was still not talking. Virgil asked him again if he should stay with the group and this time Frank said no and told him to finish his grub and ride out. He said, "Find the road to Clarkstown or don't bother coming back, because there would be no use of having you around."

So Virgil and Joe Dean rode out about fifteen minutes ahead of the others. When they split up Virgil worked his way deeper into the foothills to look for some kind of a road. He crossed brush slopes and arroyos, holding to a south-southeast course, but he didn't see anything that resembled even a foot path. It was a few hours after leaving the group, about three o'clock in the afternoon, that Virgil came across the Indian and it was the damnedest thing he'd ever seen in his life.

There he was out in the middle of nowhere sitting at the shady edge of a mesquite thicket wrapped in an army blanket. A real Apache Indian, red headband and all and even with some paint on his face and a staff or something that was sticking out of the bushes. It looked like a fishing pole. That was the first thing Virgil thought of: an Apache Indian out in the desert fishing in a mesquite patch—the damnedest thing he'd ever seen.

Virgil said, "Hey, Indin, you sabe English any?"

Raymond San Carlos remained squatted on the ground. He nodded once.

"I'm looking for the road to Clarkstown."

Raymond shook his head now. "I don't know."

"You speak pretty good. Tell me something, what're you doing out here?"

"I'm not doing nothing."

"You live around here?"

Raymond pointed off to the side. "Not far."

"How come you got that paint on your face?"

"I just put it there."

"How come if you live around here you don't know where Clarkstown is?"

"I don't know."

"Jesus, you must be a dumb Indin. Have you seen anybody else come through here today?"

"Nobody."

"You haven't seen me, have you?"

"What?"

"You haven't seen nobody and you haven't seen me either."

Raymond said nothing.

"I don't know," Virgil said now. "Some sheriff's people ask you you're liable to tell them, aren't you? You got family around here?"

"Nobody else."

"Just you all alone. Nobody would miss you then, would they? Listen, buddy, I don't mean anything personal, but I'm afraid you seeing me isn't a good idea. I'm going to have to shoot you."

Raymond stood up now, slowly.

"You can run if you want," Virgil said, "or you can stand there and take it, I don't care; but don't start hollering and carrying on. All right?"

Virgil was wearing a shoulder rig under his coat. He looked down as he unbuttoned the one button, drew a .44 Colt and looked up to see something coming at him and gasped as if the wind was knocked out of him as he grabbed hold of the fishing pole sticking out of his chest and saw the Indian standing there watching him and saw the sky and the sun, and that was all.

Raymond dragged Virgil's body into the mesquite. He left his spear in there too. He had two revolvers, a Winchester rifle and a horse. He didn't need a spear any more.

Joe Dean's horse smelled water. He was sure of it, so he let the animal have its head and Joe Dean went along for the ride—down into a wide canyon that was green and yellow with spring growth. When he saw the cottonwoods and then the round soft shape of the willows against the canyon slope, Joe Dean patted the horse's neck and guided him with the reins again.

It was a still pool, but not stagnant, undercutting a shelf of rock and mirroring the cliffs and canyon walls. Joe Dean dismounted. He led his horse down a bank of shale to the pool, then went belly-down at the edge and drank with his face in the water. He drank all he wanted before emptying the little bit left in his canteen and filling it to the top. Then he stretched out and drank again. He wished he had time to strip off his clothes and dive in. But he had better get the others first or Frank would see he'd bathed and start kicking and screaming again. Once he got them here they would probably all want to take a bath. That would be something, Norma in there with them, grabbing some of her under the water when Frank wasn't looking. Then she'd get out and lie up there on the bank to dry off in the sun. Nice soft white body—

Joe Dean was pushing himself up, looking at the pool and aware now of the reflections in the still water: the slope of the canyon wall high above, the shelf of rock behind him, sandy brown, and something else, something dark that resembled a man's shape, and he felt that cold prickly feeling up between his shoulder blades to his neck.

It was probably a crevice, shadowed inside. It couldn't be a man. Joe Dean got to his feet, then turned around and looked up.

Harold Jackson—bare to the waist, and a blanket over one shoulder, with his beard and tribal scars and streak of white paint—stood looking down at him from the rock shelf.

"How you doing?" Harold said. "You get enough water?"

Joe Dean stared at him. He didn't answer right away. God, no. He was thinking and trying to decide quickly if it was a good thing or a bad thing to be looking up at Harold Jackson at a water hole in the Little Ajo Mountains.

He said finally, "How'd you get here?"

"Same way you did."

"You got away after we left?"

"Looks like it, don't it?"

"Well, that must've been something. Just you?"

"No, Raymond come with me."

"I don't see him. Where is he?"

"He's around some place."

"If there wasn't any horses left, how'd you get here?"

"How you think?"

"I'm asking you, Sambo."

"We run, Joe."

"You're saying you run here all the way from Sentinel?"

"Well, we stop last night," Harold said, and kept watching him. "Up in the Crater Mountains."

"Is that right? We camped up there too."

"I know you did," Harold said.

Joe Dean was silent for a long moment before he said, "You killed Howard and Dancey, didn't you?"

"No, we never killed them. We let them go."

"What do you want?"

"Not you, Joe. Unless you want to take part."

Joe Dean's revolver was in his belt. He didn't see a gun or a knife or anything on Harold, just the blanket over his shoulder and covering his arm. It looked like it would be pretty easy. So he drew his revolver.

As he did, though, Harold pulled the blanket across his body with his left hand. His right hand came up holding Howard Crowder's .44 and he shot Joe Dean with it three times in the chest. And now Harold had two revolvers, a rifle, and a horse. He left Joe Dean lying next to the pool for Shelby to find.

They had passed Clarkstown, Shelby decided. Missed it. Which meant they were still in the Little Ajo Mountains, past the chance of having a sit-down hot meal today, but that much closer to the border. That part was all right. What bothered him, they had not seen Virgil or Joe Dean since noon.

It was almost four o'clock now. Junior and Soonzy were riding ahead about thirty yards. Norma was keeping up with Shelby, staying close, afraid of him but more afraid of falling behind and finding herself alone. If Shelby didn't know where they were, Norma knew that she, by herself, would never find her way out. She had no idea why Shelby had brought her, other than at Virgil's request to have a woman along. No one had approached her in the camp last night. She knew, though, once they were across the border and the men relaxed and quit looking behind them, one of them, probably Virgil, would come to her with that fixed expression on his face and she would take him on and be nice to him as long as she had no other choice.

"We were through here one time," Shelby said. "We went up through Copper Canyon to Clarkstown the morning we went after the Cornelia Mine payroll. I don't see any familiar sights, though. It all looks the same."

She knew he wasn't speaking to her directly. He was thinking out loud, or stoking his confidence with the sound of his own voice.

"From here what we want to hit is Growler Pass," Shelby said. "Top the pass and we're at Bates Well. Then we got two ways to go. Southeast to Dripping Springs and on down to Sonoyta. Or a shorter trail to the border through Quitobaquito. I haven't decided yet which way we'll go. When Virgil comes in I'll ask him if Billy Santos said anything about which trail's best this time of the year."

"What happened to the two men last night?" Norma asked him.

Shelby didn't answer. She wasn't sure if she should ask him again. Before she could decide, Junior was riding back toward them and Shelby had reined in to wait for him.

Junior was grinning. "I believe Joe Dean's found us some water. His tracks lead into that canyon yonder and it's chock-full of green brush and willow trees."

"There's a tank somewhere in these hills," Shelby said.

"Well, I believe we've found it," Junior said.

They found the natural tank at the end of the canyon. They found Joe Dean lying with his head and outstretched arms in the still water. And they found planted in the sand next to him, sticking straight up, a spear made of a bamboo fishing pole and a mortar trowel.

13

———•◆•———

They camped on high ground south of Bates Well and in the morning came down through giant saguaro country, down through a hollow in the hills to within sight of Quitobaquito.

There it was, a row of weathered adobes and stock pens beyond a water hole that resembled a shallow, stagnant lake—a worn-out village on the bank of a dying pool that was rimmed with rushes and weeds and a few stunted trees.

Shelby didn't like it.

He had pictured a green oasis and found a dusty, desert water hole. He had imagined a village where they could trade for food and fresh horses, a gateway to Mexico with the border lying not far beyond the village, across the Rio Sonoyta.

He didn't like the look of the place. He didn't like not seeing any people over there. He didn't like the open fifty yards between here and the water hole.

He waited in a cover of rocks and brush with Norma and Junior and Soonzy behind him, and Mexico waiting less than a mile away. They could go around Quitobaquito. But if they did, where was the next water? The Sonoyta could be dried up, for all he knew. They could head for Santo Domingo, a fair-sized town that shouldn't be too far away. But what if they missed it? There was water right in front of them and, goddamn-it, they were going to have some, all they wanted. But he hesitated, studying the village, waiting for some sign of life other than a dog barking, and remembering Joe Dean with the three bullets in his chest.

Junior said, "Jesus, are we gong to sit here in the sun all day?"

"I'll let you know," Shelby said.

"You want me to get the water?"

"I did, I would have told you."

"Well, then tell me, goddamn-it. You think I'm scared to?"

Soonzy settled it. He said, "I think maybe everybody's off some place to a wedding or something. That's probably what it is. These people, somebody dies or gets married, they come from all over."

"Maybe," Shelby said.

"I don't see no other way but for me to go in there and find out. What do you say, Frank?"

After a moment Shelby nodded. "All right, go take a look."

"If it's the nigger and the Indin," Soonzy said, "if they're in there, I'll bring 'em out."

Raymond held the wooden shutter open an inch, enough so he could watch Soonzy coming in from the east end of the village, mounted, a rifle across his lap. Riding right in, Raymond thought. Dumb, or sure of himself, or maybe both. He could stick a .44 out the window and shoot him as he went by. Except that it would be a risk. He couldn't afford to miss and have Soonzy shooting in here. Raymond let the shutter close.

He pressed a finger to his lips and turned to the fourteen people, the men and women and children who were huddled in the dim room, sitting on the floor and looking up at him now, watching silently, even the two smallest children. The people were Mexican and Papago. They wore white cotton and cast-off clothes. They had lived here all their lives and they were used to armed men riding through Quitobaquito. Raymond had told them these were bad men coming who might steal from them and harm them. They believed him and they waited in silence. Now they could hear the horse's hoofs on the hard-packed street. Raymond stood by the door with a revolver in his hand. The sound of the horse passed. Raymond waited, then opened the door a crack and looked out. Soonzy was nowhere in sight.

If anybody was going to shoot at anybody going for water, Soonzy decided, it would have to be from one of the adobes facing the water hole. There was a tree in the backyard of the first one that would block a clear shot across the hole. So that left him only two places to search—two low-roofed, crumbling adobes that stood bare in the sunlight, showing their worn bricks and looking like part of the land.

Soonzy stayed close to the walls on the front side of the street. When he came to the first adobe facing the water hole, he reached down to push the door open, ducked his head, and walked his horse inside.

He came out into the backyard on foot, holding a revolver now, and seeing just one end of the water hole because the tree was in the way. From the next adobe, though, a person would have a clear shot. There weren't any side windows, which was good. It let Soónzy walk right up to the place. He edged around the corner, following his revolver to the back door and got right up against the boards so he could listen. He gave himself time; there was no hurry. Then he was glad he did when the sound came from inside, a little creaking sound, like a door or a window being opened.

Harold eased open the front door a little more. He still couldn't see anything. The man had been down at the end of the street, coming this way on his horse big as anything, and now he was gone. He looked down half a block and across the street, at the adobe, where Raymond was waiting with the people, keeping them quiet and out of the way. He saw Raymond coming out; Harold wanted to wave to him to get inside. What was he doing?

The back door banged open and Soonzy was standing in the room covering him with a Colt revolver.

"Got you," Soonzy said. "Throw the gun outside and turn this way. Where's that red nigger at?"

"You mean Raymond?" Harold said. "He left. I don't know where he went."

"Which one of you shot Joe Dean, you or him?"

"I did. I haven't seen Raymond since before that."

"What'd you do with Virgil?"

"I don't think I know any Virgil."

"Frank's brother. He took us off the train."

"I haven't seen him."

"You want me to pull the trigger?"

"I guess you'll pull it whether I tell or not." Harold felt the door behind him touch the heel of his right foot. He had not moved the foot, but now he felt the door push gently against it.

"I'll tell Frank Shelby," Harold said then. "How'll that be? You take me to Frank I'll tell him where his brother is and them other two boys. But if you shoot me he won't ever know where his brother's at, will he? He's liable to get mad at somebody."

Soonzy had to think about that. He wasn't going to be talked into anything he didn't want to do. He said, "Whether I shoot you now or later you're still going to be dead."

"It's up to you," Harold said.

"All right, turn around and open the door."

"Yes-suh, captain," Harold said.

He opened the door and stepped aside and Raymond, in the doorway, fired twice and hit Soonzy dead center both times.

Shelby and Junior and Norma Davis heard the shots. They sounded far off, but the reports were thin and clear and unmistakable. Soonzy had gone into the village. Two shots were fired and Soonzy had not come out. They crouched fifty yards from water with empty canteens and the border less than a mile away.

Norma said they should go back to Bates Well. They could be there by evening, get water, and take the other trail south.

And run into a posse coming down from Gila, Shelby said. They didn't have time enough even to wait here till dark. They had to go with water or go without it, but they had to go, now.

So Junior said Jesus, give me the goddamn canteens or we will be here all day. He said maybe those two could paint theirselves up and bushwack a man, but he would bet ten dollars gold they couldn't shoot worth a damn for any distance. He'd get the water and be back in a minute. Shelby told Junior he would return fire and cover him if they started shooting, and Junior said that was mighty big of him.

"There," Raymond said. "You see him?"

Harold looked out past the door frame to the water hole. "Whereabouts?"

Raymond was at the window of the adobe. "He worked his way over to the right, coming in on the other side of the tree. You'll see him in a minute."

"Which one?"

"It looked like Junior."

"He can't sit still, can he?"

"I guess he's thirsty," Raymond said. "There he is. He thinks that tree's hiding him."

Harold could see him now, over to the right a little, approaching the bank of the water hole, running across the open in a hunch-shouldered crouch, keeping his head down behind nothing.

"How far do you think?" Raymond said.

Harold raised his Winchester and put the front sight on Junior. "Hundred yards, a little more."

"Can you hit him?"

Harold watched Junior slide down the sandy bank and begin filling the canteens, four of them, kneeling in the water and filling them one at a time. "Yeah, I can hit him," Harold said, and he was thinking, He's taking too long. He should fill them all at once, push them under and hold them down.

"What do you think?" Raymond said.

"I don't know."

"He ever do anything to you?"

"He done enough."

"I don't know either," Raymond said.

"He'd kill you. He wouldn't have to think about it."

"I guess he would."

"He'd enjoy it."

"I don't know," Raymond said. "It's different, seeing him when he don't see us."

"Well," Harold said, "if he gets the water we might not see him again. We might not see Frank Shelby again either. You want Frank?"

"I guess so."

"I do too," Harold said.

They let Junior come up the bank with the canteens, up to the rim before they shot him. Both fired at once and Junior slid back down to the edge of the still pool.

Norma looked at it this way: they would either give up, or they would be killed. Giving up would be taking a chance. But it would be less chancey if she gave up on her own, without Shelby. After all, Shelby had forced her to come along and that was a fact, whether the Indian and the Negro realized it or not. She had never been really unkind to them in prison; she had had nothing to do with them. So there was no reason for them to harm her now—once she explained she was more on their side than on Frank's. If they were feeling mean and had rape on their mind, well, she could handle that easily enough.

There was one canteen left, Joe Dean's. Norma picked it up and waited for Shelby's reaction.

"They'll shoot you too," he said.

"I don't think so."

"Why, because you're a woman?"

"That might help."

"God Almighty, you don't know them, do you?"

"I know they've got nothing against me. They're mad at you, Frank, not me."

"They've killed six people we know of. You just watched them gun Junior—and you're going to walk out there in the open?"

"Do you believe I might have a chance?"

Shelby paused. "A skinny one."

"Skinny or not, it's the only one we have, isn't it?"

"You'd put your life up to help me?"

"I'm just as thirsty as you are."

"Norma, I don't know—two days ago you were trying to turn me in."

"That's a long story, and if we get out of here we can talk about it sometime, Frank."

"You really believe you can do it."

"I want to so bad."

Boy, she was something. She was a tough, good-looking woman, and by God, maybe she could pull it. Frank said, "It might work. You know it?"

"I'm going way around to the side," Norma said, "where those bushes are. Honey, if they start shooting—"

"You're going to make it, Norma, I know you are. I got a feeling about this and I *know* it's going to work." He gave her a hug and rubbed his hand gently up and down her back, which was damp with perspiration. He said, "You hurry back now."

Norma said, "I will, sweetheart."

Watching her cross the open ground, Shelby got his rifle up between a notch in the rocks and put it on the middle adobe across the water hole. Norma was approaching from the left, the same way Junior had gone in, but circling wider than Junior had, going way around and now approaching the pool where tall rushes grew along the bank. Duck down in there, Shelby said. But Norma kept going, circling the water hole, following the bank as it curved around toward the far side. Jesus, she had nerve; she was heading for the bushes almost to the other side. But then she was past the bushes. She was running. She was into the yard where the big tree stood before Shelby said, "Goddamn you!" out loud, and swung his Winchester on the moving figure in the striped skirt. He fired and levered and fired two more before they opened up from the house and he had to go down behind the rocks. By the time he looked again she was inside.

* * *

Frank Shelby gave up an hour later. He waved a flour sack at them for a while, then brought the three horses down out of the brush and led them around the water hole toward the row of adobes. He had figured out most of what he was going to say. The tone was the important thing. Take them by surprise. Bluff them. Push them off balance. They'd expect him to run and hide, but instead he was walking up to them. He could talk to them. Christ, a dumb nigger and an Indin who'd been taking orders and saying yes-sir all their lives. They had run scared from the train and had been scared into killing. That's what happened. They were scared to death of being caught and taken back to prison. So he would have to be gentle with them at first and calm them down, the way you'd calm a green horse that was nervous and skittish. There, there, boys, what's all this commotion about? Show them he wasn't afraid, and gradually take charge. Take care of Norma also. God, he was dying to get his hands on Norma.

Harold and Raymond came out of the adobe first, with rifles, though not pointing them at him. Norma came out behind them and moved over to the side, grinning at him, goddamn her. It made Shelby mad, though it didn't hold his attention. Harold and Raymond did that with their painted faces staring at him; no expression, just staring, waiting for him.

As he reached the yard Shelby grinned and said, "Boys, I believe it's about time we cut out this foolishness. What do you say?"

Harold and Raymond waited.

Shelby said, "I mean what are we doing shooting at each other for? We're on the same side. We spent months together in that hell hole on the bluff and, by Jesus, we jumped the train together, didn't we?"

Harold and Raymond waited.

Shelby said, "If there was some misunderstanding you had with my men we can talk about it later because, boys, right now I believe we should get over that border before we do any more standing around talking."

And Harold and Raymond waited.

Shelby did too, a moment. He said then, "Have I done anything to you? Outside of a little pissy-ass difference we had, haven't I always treated you boys fair? What do you want from me? You want me to pay you something? I'll tell you what, I'll pay you both to hire on and ride with me. What do you say?"

Harold Jackson said, "You're going to ride with us, man. Free."

"To where?"

"Back to Sentinel."

Norma started laughing as Shelby said, "Jesus, are you crazy? What are you talking about, back to Sentinel? You mean back to *prison*?"

"That's right," Harold said. "Me and Raymond decide that's the thing you'd like the worst."

She stopped laughing altogether as Raymond said, "You're going too, lady."

"Why?" Norma looked dazed, taken completely by surprise. "I'm not with him. What have I ever done to you?"

"Nobody has ever done anything to us," Raymond said to Harold. "Did you know that?"

The section gang that arrived from Gila told Mr. Manly no, they had not heard any news yet. There were posses out from the Sand Tank Mountains to the Little Ajos, but nobody had reported seeing anything. At least it had not been reported to the railroad.

They asked Mr. Manly how long he had been here at Sentinel and he told them five days, since the escape. He didn't tell them Mr. Rynning had wired and instructed him to stay. "You have five days," Mr. Rynning said. "If the convict pair you released do not return, report same to the sheriff, Maricopa. Report in person to me."

Mr. Manly took that to mean he was to wait here five full days and leave the morning of the sixth. The first two days there had been a mob here. Railroad people with equipment, a half-dozen guards that had been sent over from Florence, and the Maricopa sheriff, who had been here getting statements and the descriptions of the escaped convicts. He had told the Maricopa sheriff about sending out the two trackers and the man had said, trackers? Where did you get trackers? He told him and the man had stared at him with a funny look. It was the sheriff who must have told Mr. Rynning about Harold and Raymond.

The railroad had sent an engine with a crane to lift the locomotive and the baggage car onto the track. Then the train had to be pulled all the way to the yard at Gila, where a new locomotive was hooked up and the prisoners were taken on to Florence. There had certainly been a lot of excitement those two days. Since then the place had been deserted except for the telegrapher and the section gang. They were usually busy and it gave Mr. Manly time to think of what he would tell Mr. Rynning.

It wasn't an easy thing to explain: trusting two convicts enough to let them go off alone. Two murderers, Mr. Rynning would say. Yes, that was true; but he had still trusted them. And until this morning he had expected to see them again. That was the sad part. He sincerely believed he had made progress with Harold and Raymond. He believed he had taught them something worthwhile about life, about living with their fellowman. But evidently he had been wrong. Or, to look at it honestly, he had failed. Another failure after forty years of failures.

He was in the station house late in the afternoon of the fifth day, talking to the telegrapher, passing time. Neither had spoken for a while when the telegrapher said, "You hear something?" He went to the window and said, "Riders coming in." After a pause he said, "Lord in heaven!" And Mr. Manly knew.

He was off the bench and outside, standing there waiting for them, grinning, beaming, as they rode up: his Apache and his Zulu—thank you, God, just look at them!—bringing in Frank Shelby and the woman with ropes around their necks, bringing them in tied fast and making Mr. Manly, at this moment, the happiest man on earth.

Mr. Manly said, "I don't believe it. Boys, I am looking at it and I don't believe it. Do you know there are posses all over the country looking for these people?"

"We passed some of them," Raymond said.

"They still after the others?"

"I guess they are," Raymond said.

"Boys, I'll tell you, I've been waiting here for days, worried sick about you. I even began to wonder—I hate to say it but it's true—I even began to wonder if you were coming back. Now listen, I want to hear all about it, but first I want to say this. For what you've done here, for your loyalty and courage, risking your lives to bring these people back—which you didn't even have to do—I am going to personally see that you're treated like white men at Florence and are given decent work to do."

The Apache and the Zulu sat easily in their saddles watching Mr. Manly, their painted faces staring at him without expression.

"I'll tell you something else," Mr. Manly said. "You keep your record clean at Florence, I'll go before the prison board myself and make a formal request that your sentences be commuted, which means cut way down." Mr. Manly was beaming. He said, "Fellas, what do you think of that?"

They continued to watch him until Harold Jackson the Zulu, leaning on his saddle horn, said to Mr. Manly, "Fuck you, captain."

They let go of the ropes that led to Frank Shelby and the woman. They turned their horses in tight circles and rode out, leaving a mist of fine dust hanging in the air.

Turn the page for a sneak preview
of Elmore Leonard's

LAST STAND AT SABER RIVER

———◆———

Paul Cable sat hunched forward at the edge of the pine shade, his boots crossed and his elbows supported on his knees. He put the field glasses to his eyes again and, four hundred yards down the slope, the two-story adobe was brought suddenly, silently before him.

This was The Store. It was Denaman's. It was a plain, tan-pink southern Arizona adobe with a wooden loading platform, but no *ramada* to hold off the sun. It was the only general supply store from Hidalgo north to Fort Buchanan; and until the outbreak of the war it had been a Hatch & Hodges swing station.

The store was familiar and it was good to see, because it meant Cable and his family were almost home. Martha was next to him, the children were close by; they were anxious to be home after two and a half years away from it. But the sight of a man Cable had never seen before—a man with one arm—had stopped them.

He stood on the loading platform facing the empty sunlight of the yard, staring at the willow trees that screened the river close beyond the adobe, his right hand on his hip, his left sleeve tucked smoothly, tightly into his waist. Above him, the faded, red-lettered *Denaman's Store* inscription extended the full width of the adobe's double doors.

Cable studied the man. There was something about him.

Perhaps because he had only one arm. No, Cable thought then, that made you think of the war, the two and a half years of it, but you felt something before you saw he had only one arm.

Then he realized it was the habit of surviving formed during two and a half years of war. The habit of not trusting any movement he could not immediately identify. The habit of not walking into anything blindly. He had learned to use patience and weigh alternatives and to be sure of a situation before he acted. As sure as he could be in his own mind.

Now Cable's glasses moved over the wind-scarred face of the adobe, following the one-armed man's gaze to the grove of willows and the river hidden beyond the hanging screen of branches.

A girl came out of the trees carrying a bucket and Cable said, "There's Luz again. Here—" He handed the glasses to his wife who was kneeling, sitting back on her legs, one hand raised to shield her eyes from the sun glare.

Martha Cable raised the glasses. After a moment she said, "It's Luz Acaso. But still it doesn't seem like Luz."

"All of a sudden she's a grown-up woman," Cable said. "She'd be eighteen now."

"No," Martha said. "It's something else. Her expression. The way she moves."

Through the glasses, the girl crossed the yard leisurely. Her eyes were lowered and did not rise until she reached the platform and started up the steps. When she looked up her face was solemn and warm brown in the sunlight. Martha remembered Luz's knowing eyes and her lips that were always softly parted, ready to smile or break into laughter. But now she wore an expression of weariness. Her eyes went to the man on the platform, then away from him quickly as he glanced at her and she passed into the store.

She's tired, or ill, Martha thought. Or afraid.

"She went inside?" Cable asked.

The glasses lowered briefly and Martha nodded. "But he's still there. Cable, for some reason I think she's afraid of him."

"Maybe." He watched Martha concentrating on the man on the platform. "But why, if Denaman's there?"

"If he's there," Martha said.

"Where else would he be?"

"I was going to ask the same question."

"Well, let's take it for granted he's inside."

"And Manuel?" She was referring to Luz's brother.

"Manuel could be anywhere."

Martha was still watching the man on the platform, studying him so that an impression of him would be left in her mind. He was a tall man, heavy boned, somewhat thin with dark hair and mustache. He was perhaps in his late thirties. His left arm was off between the shoulder and the elbow.

"I suppose he was in the war," Martha said.

"Probably." Cable nodded thoughtfully. "But which

side?" That's something, Cable said to himself. You don't trust him. Any man seen from a distance you dislike and distrust. It's good to be careful, but you could be carrying it too far.

Briefly he thought of John Denaman, the man who had given him his start ten years before and talked him into settling in the Saber River valley. It would be good to see John again. And it would be good to see Luz, to talk to her, and Manuel. His good friend Manuel. Luz and Manuel's father had worked for Denaman until a sudden illness took his life. After that, John raised both of them as if they were his own children.

"Now he's going inside," Martha said.

Cable waited. After a moment he turned, pushing himself up, and saw his daughter standing only a few feet away. Clare was six, their oldest child: a quiet little girl with her mother's dark hair and eyes and showing signs of developing her mother's clean-lined, easily remembered features; resembling her mother just as the boys favored their father. She stood uncertainly with her hands clutched to her chest.

"Sister, you round up the boys."

"Are we going now?"

"In a minute."

He watched her run back into the trees and in a moment he heard a boy's shrill voice. That would be Davis, five years old. Sandy, not yet four, would be close behind his brother, following every move Davis made; almost every move.

Cable brought his sorrel gelding out of the trees and stepped into the saddle. "He'll come out again when he hears me," Cable said. "But wait till you see us talking before you come down. All right?"

Martha nodded. She smiled faintly, saying, "He'll probably turn out to be an old friend of John Denaman's."

"Probably."

Cable nudged the sorrel with his heels and rode off down the yellow sweep of hillside, sitting erect and tight to the saddle with his right knee touching the stock of a Spencer carbine, his right elbow feeling the Walker Colt on his hip, and keeping his eyes on the adobe now, thinking: This could be a scout. This could be the two and a half years still going on. . . .

As soon as he had made up his mind to enlist he had sold his stock, all of his cattle, all two hundred and fifty head, and all but three of his horses. He had put Martha and the children in the wagon and taken them to Sudan, Texas, to the home of Martha's parents. He did this because he believed deeply in the Confederacy, as he believed in his friends who had gone to fight for it.

Because of a principle he traveled from the Saber River, Arizona Territory, to Chattanooga, Tennessee, taking with him a shotgun, a revolving pistol and two horses; and there on June 21, 1862, he joined J. A. Wharton's 8th Texas Cavalry, part of Nathan Bedford Forrest's command.

Three weeks later Cable saw his first action and received his first wound during Forrest's raid on Murfreesboro. On September 3, Paul Cable was commissioned a captain and appointed to General Forrest's escort. From private to captain in less than three months; those things happened in Forrest's command. Wounded twice again after Murfreesboro; the third and final time on November 28, 1864, at a place called Huey's Mills—shot from his saddle as they crossed the Duck River to push Wilson's Union Cavalry back to Franklin, Tennessee. Cable, with gunshot wounds in his left hip and thigh, was taken to the hospital at Columbia. On December 8 he was told to go home "the best way you know how." There were more seriously wounded men who needed his cot; there would be a flood of them soon, with General Hood about to pounce on the Yankees at Nashville. Go home, he was told, and thank God for your gunshot wounds.

So for Cable the war was over, though it was still going on in the east and the feeling of it was still with him. He was not yet thirty, a lean-faced man above average height and appearing older after his service with Nathan Bedford Forrest: after Chickamauga, had come Fort Pillow, Bryce's Crossroads, Thompson's Station, three raids into West Tennessee and a hundred nameless skirmishes. He was a calm-appearing man and the war had not changed that. A clear-thinking kind of man who had taught himself to read and write, taught himself the basic rules and his wife had helped him from there.

Martha Sanford Cable was twenty-seven now. A West Texas girl, though convent-educated in New Orleans. Seven years before she had left Sudan to come to the Saber River as Paul Cable's wife, to help him build a home and provide him with a family. . . .

Now they were returning to the home they had built with the family they had begun. They were before Denaman's Store, only four miles from their own land.

And Cable was entering the yard, still with his eyes on

the loading platform and the double doors framed in the pale wall of the adobe, reining in his sorrel and approaching at a walk.

The right-hand door opened and the man with one arm stepped out to the platform. He walked to the edge of it and stood with his thumb in his belt looking down at Cable.

Cable came on. He kept his eyes on the man, but said nothing until he had pulled to a halt less than ten feet away. From the saddle, Cable's eyes were even with the man's knees.

"John Denaman inside?"

The man's expression did not change. "He's not here any more."

"He moved?"

"You could say that."

"Maybe I should talk to Luz," Cable said.

The man's sunken cheeks and the full mustache covering the line of his mouth gave his face a hard, bony expression, but it was not tensed. He said, "You know Luz?"

"Since she was eight years old," Cable answered. "Since the day I first set foot in this valley."

"Well, now—" The hint of a smile altered the man's gaunt expression. "You wouldn't be Cable, would you?"

Cable nodded.

"Home from the wars." The man still seemed to be smiling. "Luz's mentioned you and your family. Her brother too. He tells how you and him fought off Apaches when they raided your stock."

Cable nodded. "Where's Manuel now?"

"Off somewhere." The man paused. "You been to your place yet?"

"We're on our way."

"You've got a surprise coming."

Cable watched him, showing little curiosity. "What does that mean?"

"You'll find out."

"I think you're changing the subject," Cable said mildly. "I asked you what happened to John Denaman."

For a moment the man said nothing. He turned then and called through the open door, "Luz, come out here!"

Cable watched him. He saw the man's heavy-boned face turn to look down at him again, and almost immediately the Mexican girl appeared in the doorway. Cable's hand went to the curled brim of his hat.

"Luz, honey, you're a welcome sight." He said it warmly, and he wanted to jump up on the platform and kiss her but the presence of this man stopped him.

"Paul—"

He saw the surprise in the expression of her mouth and in her eyes, but it was momentary and she returned his gaze with a smile that was grave and without joy, a smile that vanished the instant the man with one arm spoke.

"Luz, tell him what happened to Denaman."

"You haven't told him?" She looked at Cable quickly, then seemed to hesitate. "Paul, he's dead. He died almost a year ago."

"Nine months," the man with one arm said. "I came here the end of August. He died the month before."

Cable's eyes were on the man, staring at him, feeling

now that he had known Denaman was dead, had sensed it from the way the man had spoken—from the tone of his voice.

"You could have come right out and told me," Cable said.

"Well, you know now."

"Like you were making a game out of it."

The man stared down at Cable indifferently. "Why don't you just let it go?"

"Paul," Luz said, "it came unexpectedly. He wasn't sick."

"His heart?"

Luz nodded. "He collapsed shortly after noon and by that evening he was dead."

"And you happened to come a month later," Cable said, looking at the man again.

"Why don't you ask what I'm doing here?" The man looked up at the sound of the double team wagon on the grade, his eyes half closed in the sunlight, his gaze holding on the far slope now. "That your family?"

"Wife and three youngsters," Cable said.

The man's gaze came down. "You made a long trip for nothing." He seemed about to smile, though he was not smiling now.

"All right," Cable said. "Why?"

"Some men are living in your house."

"If there are, they're about to move."

The smile never came, but the man stared down at Cable intently. "Come inside and I'll tell you about it." Then he turned abruptly, though he glanced again at the approaching wagon before going into the store.

Cable could hear the jingling, creaking sound of the wagon closer now, but he kept his eyes on Luz until she looked at him.

"Luz, who is he?"

"His name is Edward Janroe."

"The man acts like he owns the place."

Her eyes rose briefly. "He does. Half of it."

"But why—"

"Are you coming?" Janroe was in the doorway. He was looking at Cable and with a nod of his head indicated Luz. "You got to drag things out of her. I've found it's more trouble than it's worth." He waited until Cable stirred in the saddle and began to dismount. "I'll be inside," he said, and stepped away from the door.

Cable dropped his reins, letting them trail. He swung down and mounted the steps to the platform. For a moment he watched Luz Acaso in silence.

"Are you married to him?"

"No."

"But he's been living here eight months and has a half interest in the store."

"You think what you like."

"I'm not thinking anything. I want to know what's going on."

"He'll tell you whatever you want to know."

"Luz, do you think I'm being nosy? I want to help you."

"I don't need help." She was looking beyond him, watching the wagon entering the yard.

All right, he thought, don't push her. It occurred to

him then that Martha was the one to handle Luz. Why keep harping at her and get her nervous. Martha could soothe the details out of her in a matter of minutes.

Cable patted her shoulder and stepped past her into the abrupt dimness of the store.

He moved down the counter that lined the front wall, his hand gliding down the worn, shiny edge of it and his eyes roaming over the almost bare shelves. There were scattered rows of canned goods, bolts of material, work clothes, boxes that told nothing of their contents. Above, Rochester lamps hanging from a wooden beam, buckets and bridles and coils of rope. Most of the goods on the shelves had the appearance of age, as if they had been here a long time.

Cable's eyes lowered and he almost stopped, unexpectedly seeing Janroe beyond the end of the counter in the doorway to the next room. Janroe was watching him closely.

"You walk all right," Janroe said mildly. "Not a mark on you that shows; but they wouldn't have let you go without a wound."

"It shows if I walk far enough," Cable said. "Or if I stay mounted too long."

"That sounds like the kind of wound to have. Where'd you get it?"

"On the way to Nashville."

"With Hood?"

"In front of him. With Forrest."

"You're a lucky man. I mean to be in one piece."

"I suppose."

"Take another case. I was with Kirby Smith from the summer of sixty-one to a year later when we marched up to Kentucky River toward Lexington. Near Richmond we met a Yankee general named Bull Nelson." Janroe's eyes narrowed and he grinned faintly, remembering the time. "He just had recruits, a pick-up army, and I'll tell you we met them good. Cut clean the hell through them, and the ones we didn't kill ran like you never saw men run in your life. The cavalry people mopped up after that and we took over four thousand prisoners that one afternoon."

Janroe paused and the tone of his voice dropped. "But there was one battery of theirs on a ridge behind a stone fence. I was taking some men up there to get them . . . and the next day I woke up in a Richmond field hospital without an arm."

He was watching Cable closely. "You see what I mean? We'd licked them. The fight was over and put away. But because of this one battery not knowing enough to give up, or too scared to, I lost a good arm."

But you've got one left and you're out of the war, so why don't you forget about it, Cable thought, and almost said it; but instead he nodded, looking at the shelves.

"Maybe Luz told you I was in the army," Janroe said.

"No, only your name, and that you own part of the store."

"That's a start. What else do you want to know?"

"Why you're here."

"You just said it. Because I own part of the store."

"Then how you came to be here."

"You've got a suspicious mind."

"Look," Cable said quietly, "John Denaman was a friend of mine. He dies suddenly and you arrive to buy in."

"That's right. But you want to know what killed him?"

When Cable said nothing Janroe's eyes lifted to the almost bare shelves. "He didn't have enough goods to sell. He didn't have regular money coming in. He worried, not knowing what was going to happen to his business." Janroe's gaze lowered to Cable again. "He even worried about Luz and Vern Kidston. They were keeping company and, I'm told, the old man didn't see eye to eye with Vern. Because of different politics, you might say. So it was a combination of things that killed him. Worries along with old age. And if you think it was anything else, you're going on pure imagination."

"Let's go back to Vern Kidston," Cable said. "I never heard of him; so what you're saying doesn't mean a whole lot."

Janroe's faint smile appeared. "Vern came along about two years ago, I'm told. He makes his living supplying the Union cavalry with remounts. Delivers them up to Fort Buchanan."

"He lives near here?"

"In the old Toyopa place. How far's that from you?"

"About six miles."

"They say Vern's fixed it up."

"It'd take a lot of fixing. The house was half burned down."

"Vern's got the men."

"I'll have to meet him."

"You will. You'll meet him all right."

Cable's eyes held on Janroe. "It sounds like you can hardly wait."

"There's your suspicious mind again." Janroe straightened and stepped into the next room. "Come on. It's time I poured you a drink."